"As far as we have to," Claire said, breathless, even as her voice hitched when he pressed his lips to her neck. Suddenly, she didn't care that they were being watched. "You?"

"As far as you want to go," he replied. He pressed her full against his body, so that she could not mistake the feel of his erection against her, even through the layers of her gown. "I came here with no intention beyond getting you to safety as soon as possible. But I'd be lying if I denied how beautiful you are or how hot you look in that dress, especially now that it's half-off. Making love to you would not be a hardship. In fact, it would be my pleasure."

Her jaw dropped open momentarily, then she lifted her chin and laughed. "Then I think I'm going to like working with you, Special Agent Murrieta."

"If we do it right, it won't be work. And please, call me Michael."

"By all means, Michael. Let's give those pervs behind the camera something worth watching."

Dear Reader,

I love old movies. Not all old movies, mind you. I prefer the epic, swashbuckling films where swordplay rules the day and the heroes survive not only because of their skill and speed, but also because of their irrepressible charm with the ladies. Pirate movies are a personal favorite, but I also adore stories set around the exploits of a certain black-masked bandit who rode around colonial California and fought for the rights of the downtrodden. And at the same time, he somehow managed to win a beautiful woman who really shouldn't have had anything to do with him.

Over the years, this hero has been played by many great actors, each giving him their own spin. So I thought, why not do the same with the heroes of my series, who are all fictionally descended from the real-life outlaw who supposedly inspired the legend? Three brothers couldn't be more different than wealthy, educated Alejandro (hero of *Too Hot to Touch,* August 2011), FBI agent Michael and their black sheep brother, Daniel. Each man has inherited some of their infamous ancestor's daring, bravado and charm, but all in a different way.

Recreating a historical legend in order to fit my own imagination was a true pleasure. I hope you enjoy Claire and Michael's story as much as I did writing it.

Happy Reading,

Julie Leto

Julie Leto

TOO WILD TO HOLD

TORONTO NEW YORK LONDON
AMSTERDAM PARIS SYDNEY HAMBURG
STOCKHOLM ATHENS TOKYO MILAN MADRID
PRAGUE WARSAW BUDAPEST AUCKLAND

Recycling programs
for this product may
not exist in your area.

ISBN-13: 978-0-373-79637-3

TOO WILD TO HOLD

Copyright © 2011 by Book Goddess, LLC

This edition published by arrangement with Harlequin Books S.A.

For questions and comments about the quality of this book
please contact us at Customer_eCare@Harlequin.ca.

www.Harlequin.com

Printed in U.S.A.

ABOUT THE AUTHOR

Over the course of her career, *New York Times* and *USA TODAY* bestselling author Julie Leto has published more than forty books—all of them sexy and all of them romances at heart. She shares a popular blog—www.plotmonkeys.com—with her best friends Carly Phillips, Janelle Denison and Leslie Kelly and would love for you to follow her on Twitter, where she goes by @JulieLeto. She's a born and bred Floridian homeschooling mom with a love for her family, her friends, her dachshund, her lynx-point Siamese and supersexy stories with a guaranteed happy ending.

Books by Julie Leto

To get the inside scoop on Harlequin Blaze and its talented writers, be sure to check out blazeauthors.com.

Don't miss any of our special offers. Write to us at the following address for information on our newest releases.

Harlequin Reader Service
U.S.: 3010 Walden Ave., P.O. Box 1325, Buffalo, NY 14269
Canadian: P.O. Box 609, Fort Erie, Ont. L2A 5X3

This book is dedicated to
Smarties and Kit Kat bars.

(Which means my next book will be dedicated,
once again, to Jazzercise.)

1

"DON'T MOVE. I'VE come for you—and only you."

With the whispered threat came the clamp of a man's gloved hand on the back of Claire Lécuyer's neck. She commanded herself not to flinch or alter her features, which she'd schooled into relaxed amusement. She'd entered this crowded ballroom of her own free will and she meant to leave that way, even if she had to take a madman with her.

She started to turn, but he tightened his grasp.

"You don't take orders very well," he chastised.

He didn't know the half of it.

Despite the rush of adrenaline pumping through her veins, Claire willed her voice to remain light and lilting, in keeping with the character she'd created. Tonight she wasn't just a former cop turned private investigator searching for a missing person—she was, in this undercover incarnation, a sweet Southern belle looking for her lover among the throng.

"But the night has just begun," she said. "Who knows who is going to end up with whom?"

Two hundred years had passed since the first quadroon ball, but two weeks ago, Claire had learned that the traditions of old New Orleans had been reintroduced to modern Louisiana by sexual fetishists who called themselves *Nouvelle Placage.* In a leased plantation over an hour away from the French Quarter, the group recreated the grand ballrooms and strict rules of a system that had once been the means by which rich white landowners arranged for long-term affairs with women of the *gens de couleur libre,* a light-skinned French Creole class native to pre-Americanized New Orleans.

But the people here tonight weren't re-enactors like the ones who showed up at Chalmette National Park every January to recreate the Battle of New Orleans. These modern men paid outrageous entry fees for women who would fulfill their every fantasy. They came from across the country to enjoy a weekend of anonymous sexual encounters dressed up with proper manners, old-world moral codes and romanticized dominance and submission.

In the past, the young ladies demanded homes, generous allowances, finest clothes and educations for their bastard children from the men they took as lovers. In this modern revival, the compensation was a hell of a lot more complicated. And the affairs only lasted for a weekend—which meant Claire had that long to complete her case and find Josslyn Granger.

Technically, Josslyn wasn't missing, though for four years, her whereabouts had been unknown. According to her former husband, she'd announced her defection from suburban soccer mom to sexual deviant, filed for divorce and disappeared. But though she'd granted her perplexed husband papers to dissolve their marriage, she'd conveniently forgotten to give up parental rights for their two children.

Since then, Robert Granger had hired a dozen private

investigators to search for his wayward ex-wife as she followed various sex partners and sex clubs around the country, but none had succeeded in pinning her down. When the husband heard she'd be in New Orleans for the *Nouvelle Placage* event, he'd hired Claire. Now that Granger had remarried, his job required frequent overseas travel, and his new wife, for both legal and emotional reasons, needed to adopt Josslyn's kids. But for that to happen, Claire had to find Josslyn and convince her to sign the papers she'd hidden nearby.

The case was a welcome diversion from her usual background checks and cheating spouse investigations. She liked to succeed where others had failed. She adored undercover work and relished a chance to test her own limits.

What she didn't like was being manhandled by some guy who may or may not be the stalker the FBI had warned her about. A stalker who was after Claire.

"You will end up with me," he said, his voice a low, but confident promise.

She forced a girlish giggle. If he was the stalker, maybe a different persona would throw him off. He hadn't come here expecting to find a pliant, vapid ingénue on the prowl for a man. He'd expected Claire Lécuyer—who was, in all ways, the complete opposite.

"Is that so?" she asked, her tone seemingly unconcerned. "But you have not yet negotiated my willingness to end up with you. Have you not been schooled in the ways of *Nouvelle Placage?*"

Around them, men in impeccable top coats and breeches circled the room, calculating and assessing their more-than-willing prey. From behind painted fans, women in decadent, empire-waist gowns flirted and fawned, hot with anticipation for a lover who'd soon devour them with unbridled desire and deep, deep pockets.

If not for the strains of a lively quadrille and the over-powering scent of candle wax, a stranger might mistake the scene for a modern-day masquerade. But this place was more than costumes and characters—this was the gilded antechamber into a dark and scintillating world. Claire had busted her ass to get in to this guarded community and she sure as hell wasn't going to let some mystery man derail her, no matter who he was. Maybe he was just an attendee who'd missed orientation. Or maybe he was the stalker.

Didn't matter. She wasn't dealing with her own problems until she completed her case.

"Perhaps I should call Monsieur Masterson to remind you of how things are done here?" she suggested, invoking the obviously fake name of the man who seemed to be in charge. Unfortunately, he was nowhere in sight.

"I know all the rules, Ms. Lécuyer," the mystery man assured her. "But like you, I believe that some rules are made to be broken."

She pretended to laugh, hoping to shake off her fear. "Your overconfidence does you no credit, sir. But if you are so intent on having me, perhaps you should begin by telling me who you—"

He cut off her inquiry by tightening his grip.

"You thought you'd be safe here, didn't you?" While one hand held her immobile, the other trailed up the back of her gown, brushing the beribboned stays with exquisite slowness, as if he savored a chance to untie each and every one. "You thought you could protect yourself."

Unexpectedly, his breath was tinged with the sweet scent of mint and creamy *café au lait*.

"You haven't yet proven otherwise, sir," she whispered.

Swallowing her fear, she'd pushed out the reply with a bold confidence that was only half-sincere. She didn't know very much about the man who was after her. The local FBI agents had only told her to go someplace safe and wait for contact by the lead agent who was on his way from California. Since she only had the weekend to find Josslyn Granger among the attendees of *Nouvelle Placage,* she'd figured it was as safe a place as any.

She'd had to call in quite a few favors from her days at Vice to even get in here. She'd had to pay the dues, buy the clothes, endure the orientation, all in her bid to find a woman she knew was here somewhere, but who'd yet to show. She hadn't imagined some wacked-out sicko who'd last been spotted in California would go to so much trouble to follow her.

But maybe she was wrong.

She moved her head just enough to catch a glimpse of her captor. His startling blue eyes widened, then narrowed before he tugged her back into place.

"You don't follow directions very well," he chastised.

She snorted. He wasn't the first man to utter those words to her. And he probably wouldn't be the last.

"It's one of my unique charms, I assure you."

His chuckle was low, but genuine, and soothed her anxiety rather than increased it.

"Who are you?" she asked.

"A man who caught you."

He smoothed his gloved fingers around her throat and pressed gently against her carotid artery.

Her breath hitched. Damn, damn, damn.

Why hadn't she listened more carefully to the local feds? The details she retained were sketchy. A special task force had put her name on a short list of likely victims for some creep who kidnapped women. He used the date-rape drug Rohypnol and incapacitated them long enough to act out some freakish seduction where he wore a mask and cape. Buried under by preparations for her own case, Claire had hardly given their warnings a second thought.

But then a black silk scarf embroidered with a scarlet letter Z had been delivered to her doorstep. She'd immediately taken it to the FBI, but refused their offer of protection and instead went ahead with her time-sensitive plans.

Which might, she admitted to herself now, have been a mistake.

One by one, she felt his fingers dig deeper into the skin along her throat. "One squeeze right here and you'd fall into a dead faint. A rather fashionable thing to do for young ladies of the early nineteenth century, wasn't it? No one would blink if I carried you out for a moonlight tryst."

His hand constricted, but not enough to spawn even the slightest dizziness. He was taunting her, perhaps even attempting to scare her.

And he was succeeding.

But she wasn't going down easily. She shifted her elbows into striking range when he tightened his hold again.

"Don't move," he warned.

She bit back a curse. She'd nearly dropped her cover. The women of *Nouvelle Placage* came here specifically to be manhandled. If she reacted too much like a modern-day ex-cop and not enough like a woman on the prowl, she'd have to deal with more scrutiny, more questions— more possibilities for getting tossed out on her ass.

"Let me go." She delivered the command with a honey-sweet Southern lilt, but though his grip slackened, he did not release her.

"Luckily for you, I'm not here to hurt you."

Something in his tone sliced through her suspicions, along with the fact that he loosened his hold. Maybe he wasn't the man who'd sent her the scarf. Maybe he wasn't related to the FBI case at all. Her instincts kept returning to that possibility, and though her gut had often gotten her into trouble, it had never proved wrong.

Painting on a simpering smile, she turned to face him, chin up and eyes flashing.

She didn't know him, but she'd seen him. When she'd first been paraded in the ballroom along with the other women intent on selling their services for the weekend, she'd become instantly aware of his presence.

Amid the assessing stares of the many men in attendance, his intense, sapphire blue eyes had stood out, causing a prickle of excitement to shoot through her system like liquid lightning. She'd immediately recognized the reaction. Lust. He was handsome, with a square chin and strong upper torso built more for helmets and shoulder pads than snug breeches and a fluffed cravat.

But just as quickly as she'd felt the flicker of desire, she'd dismissed it. This weekend might be all about sex for everyone else here, but she had a job to do.

Which, now that she saw her captor close up, was a crying shame.

"Of course you won't hurt me," she said, fluttering her eyelashes. "Unless I want you to, *non?*"

The corner of his mouth lifted slightly. He wanted to smile, but fought the urge. Well, that wasn't the only urge he'd have to fight tonight. He might have set his sights on her, but she had no intention of taking a lover—no matter how hypnotic his blue eyes were.

"We should negotiate our expectations in a quieter place, don't you think?" he asked.

She softened her voice to a coy purr. "I don't even know your name."

"Not yet, *ma cher*," he replied, his raspy voice scraping over her. "But I expect that, soon, you'll know much more about me than that."

Claire took a step back, dislodging his hand only for a second before he regained his touch.

"You may release me now, sir," she said.

"That would not be wise." The corner of his mouth quirked into a bold grin that liquefied her insides and gave a little tweak of desire to the tips of her tightly corseted breasts.

This was ridiculous. Why was he being so single-minded? And why was she so intrigued?

"Really? And why ever not?"

He leaned in close. His lips brushed against her curls when he spoke, but the voice that had been so accented and charming before now sliced across her skin with icy precision.

"Because you're in danger, Ms. Lécuyer, and I'm here to protect you."

2

SPECIAL AGENT MICHAEL Murrieta gave his captive a minute to let his words sink in. Once her eyes narrowed in suspicion and she visibly shed the cloying persona she'd adopted for the night, he released his hold. From the first word he'd read in her file, he'd figured she was going to be a pain in the ass, but he'd had no idea he'd have to cross the continental United States, don a crazy costume and borrow ten thousand dollars from his brother in order to find her.

He turned their bodies so that no one could see, then with practiced swiftness, flashed his credentials.

Her eyes widened and she mouthed an unspoken curse.

"Not here," she pleaded.

She took a large step back again, but he quickly regained custody of her hand. "If not here, then where, *cher?*"

His accurate Creole accent again elicited a tilted eyebrow. He had to admit that she was very good at going undercover—but he was better. He did not have her family's theater background, but Michael had years of experience with the Bureau and a partner originally from

Louisiana who'd schooled him on the accent before he'd taken off to find Claire Lécuyer and save her from a rapist.

She had not made his job easy. Only hours after alerting the local office that she had received the telltale scarf, she'd dropped off the grid and disappeared into this sexual underworld. In order to bypass their intense security on short notice, he'd had to make quick arrangements for an authentic costume—oddly, not difficult to do in New Orleans—and borrow the exorbitant entrance fee from his brother, Alejandro. He had authorization to retrieve Claire Lécuyer and put her under protective custody, but he doubted his superiors would have approved of him paying his way into a sex club.

The case hadn't yet become a major priority for the Bureau. They had serial killers to catch and homegrown terrorists to thwart. They'd only thrown the case his way because of an obscure tie between him and the rapist. But it was that same family secret that made him determined to catch this psycho before he hurt another woman. To that end, he'd finagled a consult from the Behavioral Analysis Unit at Quantico, received approval to call in Ruby, his partner, a member of his San Francisco team and was given open access to agents from the local office.

Otherwise, Michael was on his own.

It hadn't been easy to find Claire, but he'd pulled it off with limited resources and time. He had no reason to believe that her stalker, a man who'd already kidnapped and tormented five other women, wouldn't find her, too.

And when he did, Michael intended to catch him.

"So now that you have me," she said, turning up the mocking quality in her Southern belle enunciation, "whatever are you going to do with me?"

He bit back a grin, but allowed an eye roll. There was something about this woman that could drive a man to drink. Heavily. As it was, he'd taken a great risk snatching her the way he had, but he'd had a point to make. Despite FBI warnings, she'd gone off on her own. Her dossier overflowed with situations where she'd put her investigation above her own safety. She'd lost her badge for disobeying repeated orders from her superiors to stop her pursuit of a suspicious death case that had, because of her, resulted in a highly publicized murder conviction.

But he didn't see her vindication as a victory. If she'd followed procedures and worked within the system, she might have had the same result and kept her job. Not that he was one to judge at this point. He believed in the rules set forth by the Bureau which ensured that investigations were both balanced and prosecutable.

On the other hand, if he hadn't ripped a page out of her book tonight, he might never have found her before the unsub.

"The possibilities for what we might do together are endless, *cher,*" he replied, "but none would be appropriate for this company." His eyes darted to the men and women mingling around them. "Perhaps we can move along to some place a little more private?"

Within the depths of her mossy green eyes, he watched her calculate the risk versus the reward. No doubt she wanted to get rid of him as quickly as possible so she could continue to pursue her case. Had their roles been reversed, he'd want the same. But she didn't know yet what he had planned for her. If she did, she might change her mind about ditching him, which he was certain she would try to do.

Claire tilted her fan toward the foyer, then hooked

her arm into his. "This way, sir," she crooned. "If you wish to take me on, you'll first have to consult with my *maman*."

"Of course," he said, tempering a grin.

Very wisely, Claire had arranged for backup of sorts in the form of her aunt, who had stepped into the role of *maman* for the night. As the designated "mother" figure, she would negotiate a proper arrangement for her "daughter." In other words, she was the pimp. From Claire's superior smirk, she expected that her aunt would dismiss any amount Michael offered.

Well, she'd soon see that while she was wily and had come prepared, so had he.

In the grand foyer, draped sheets of sheer organza and candelabras bright with beeswax tapers masked the peeling paint and moldy smell of the old plantation house. Michael had to admire the time and effort the organizers had taken to ensure that one step over the threshold transported attendees into a different world—an old world, a racially ambiguous world when the French dominated New Orleans.

Some of the accounts he'd read during prep for this case had claimed that white men who bought quadroon women did so out of true love and affection. Glancing at Claire, with her flawless coffee-stained skin and hypnotically opaque green eyes, he could understand the appeal. How hard was it, really, to be intrigued—enslaved, even—by a woman such as her?

With her exotic beauty and impeccable manners, what man wouldn't promise away his entire legacy to possess her, even for just one night?

Michael slid his gloved hand over hers as they approached the veritable shelf of older women sitting in a row beside the open windows. A breeze scented with night-blooming jasmine cooled the air and ruffled through the swatch of silk she'd tucked into the neckline of her gown. He couldn't help but wonder what he would find if he peeled the material away—then he realized that was probably the whole point of the costume piece.

She exhaled with relief when she spotted her aunt, seated and sipping on a cocktail. Clarice had spent most of her life involved with the theater, and since she'd also been born and raised in the French Quarter, she'd easily seen more sordid events than this laced up version of consensual prostitution.

"This is my *maman*," Claire said by way of introduction, her voice lilting with confidence that he was about to be summarily dismissed.

Michael gave a low and reverent bow, took the woman's lace-gloved hand and swept a kiss across her knuckles.

"Madame," he greeted. From inside his jacket, he took out an envelope he'd prepared ahead of time.

Clarice took another sip of her drink, snatched the letter and gave it a quick, almost cursory read. Then, after looking him up and down, she nodded her approval.

"Maman!" Claire protested.

Michael fought to hide his amusement, but instead grabbed her elbow and leaned in close. "She knows who I am and she knows why I'm here. Now find us a place to talk in private or I'll drag you out and whatever case you're working on will be ruined."

Claire cast one angry look at her aunt, who smiled benignly in response. "The man makes a fair offer, my love. Go with him. Hear what he has to stay."

Claire continued to silently plead with her aunt, but the woman's matching gaze was just as stubborn and intense and Michael wasn't sure who would win this battle of wills. He had indeed sought out Claire's "guardian" shortly after spotting her in the ballroom. Following the protocol of *Nouvelle Placage,* he had revealed his credentials and verified that the aunt was helping Claire on her undercover operation, then had taken the older woman on a short stroll and explained what he'd come here to do.

Though Claire had already told her aunt about the serial rapist, she'd downgraded him to a simple stalker. So when Michael filled Aunt Clarice in on the real story, she'd agreed to help him by approving him as her niece's lover. Once alone, he and Claire could talk freely, and hopefully, Michael could convince her to leave.

For her own safety—and for her case—she had to trust him.

She muttered a very unladylike curse, and then hissed, "This way, *monsieur.*"

As THEY WALKED to the curved staircase, Claire pushed away her anger. Nothing good ever came from reacting solely on emotions. She had to concentrate on the task at hand. This FBI agent, whose name she hadn't caught as he flashed his identification, had gone to a lot of trouble not to muck up her case. The least she could do was hear him out.

Her reconnaissance at the old plantation house had been minimal, but she knew that one of the upstairs bedrooms, reserved for lovers who preferred a traditional setting rather than one of the more exotic locations throughout the house, would afford them a measure of privacy. Damn it.

She shouldn't have called the Feds about the scarf. She should have kept her mouth shut until after she'd closed her case. But she hadn't figured the government would act so quickly, not for a case where no crime against her had yet to be committed. Maybe the agent would be reasonable. Maybe he'd agree to leave her to her assignment until she'd found Josslyn and obtained the woman's signature.

Or maybe he'd already messed up her chances of bringing her case to a close by spiriting her upstairs long before any of the other women had left the dance floor.

On the second story landing, they were met by a dark-skinned woman in a plain, black dress who led them to a room at the end of the hall. Without a word, she opened the door and stood, eyes down, while they went inside. Claire had seen the woman with Masterson earlier. Was she just an employee or one of the organizers? In this world, it was impossible to know all the players.

The door shut behind them with a tight click.

Claire opened her mouth to speak, but the handsome agent held up his hand while he scanned the dimly lit room.

The boudoir did not have much furniture. A large bed with a plush comforter and an array of pillows. A silk changing screen, a chaise lounge, a small table set with a brandy decanter and two snifters, three lamps and a fireplace filled not with logs in the summer heat, but with a fragrant blaze of orange and red flowers.

Just enough scenery to evoke the weekend's theme, but not enough to detract from the real objective—sex.

When the agent looked up at an air vent in the corner, his shoulders stiffened for a split second before he turned and held out his hand with a gallant bow.

"So, *cher,* would you care to dance?"

He remained in character, so she did, too. He'd spotted

something. With her gaze cast coquettishly at her slippers, she shuffled closer. From the break in the light beneath the door, she could see that someone was listening in. She'd been warned that some of the people in the *Nouvelle Placage* entertained themselves not by participating, but by watching. Did that include eavesdropping at key holes?

After slipping her hand into the agent's, she chanced a glance at the air vent that had put him on guard.

Tucked just beyond the cast-iron scrollwork was a camera.

And from the tiny green light, she could tell it was on.

"I'd love to dance with you, sir," she said, "but we haven't any music."

"That can be rectified, I'm sure."

He marched to the door and swung it open, startling the woman hovering there.

"You!" he ordered, his manners and stature every bit as imposing as a Creole-accented Rhett Butler. "We want music. And hurry up about it."

Less than two minutes later, she wheeled in a device that looked like a gramophone, but was connected to a very modern CD player. The FBI agent practically pushed the woman out of the door, locked it, then slowly eased his fingers out of his gloves.

She did the same, but finished first as his right glove had snagged on a large emerald ring. She was just about to comment on the unusual size and style when he turned up the volume of the melodic waltz more than necessary.

He gave her a little bow, revealing a twinkle in his deep blue eyes that was not the least bit government issue.

Who was this guy?

She curtsied as she'd learned to do before she'd gotten herself kicked out of cotillion class and then willfully walked into his arms.

His hand on her waist was taut, but the one that cupped her palm was surprisingly gentle. He was a mass of contradictions, this nameless man.

"I thought the local FBI instructed you to lay low until I arrived," he said as they swayed to the string-heavy waltz.

"I don't even know who *you* are."

"Special Agent Michael Murrieta."

"Shh," she admonished. His voice was strong and would easily carry over the music. "If the room has a camera, it clearly has listening devices, too."

"These freaks aren't the only ones with hardware. I slipped an amplifier onto that gramophone. It'll boost the sound—the only thing any bugs will pick up is Mozart."

She smirked. "Actually, this is Strauss."

"It's still a cool gadget. They can watch us, but they won't hear a word we say."

She couldn't help but be impressed by both his preparedness and his slightly boyish enthusiasm for spy toys.

"Why are you here?" she asked.

"I'm the lead on your case."

"I'm not a case, Special Agent. I'm just a private citizen who turned over evidence, as instructed. But I do have my own case and I'd like to get back to it before you screw it up."

He withdrew just enough that she could see the full breadth of his cocky smirk. "Do I look like I'm screwing anything up?"

She turned her cheek, unwilling to confess that

Special Agent Michael Murrieta did appear to be incredibly competent—not to mention smooth.

He'd dressed the part of a Southern gentleman to a tee, from his polished boots to his well-fitting breeches, tapered jacket and expertly tied cravat. He'd adopted mannerisms and speech patterns of an antebellum gentleman with sparkling ease and charm, like Nathan Fillion channeling the spirit of Clark Gable.

It was disarming.

She suddenly had no trouble understanding how women could get so wrapped up in this world. The sexual allure was powerful.

At least, the sexual allure of Special Agent Michael Murrieta.

He was clearly a good actor—which meant he couldn't be trusted.

"Why are you here?" she asked, tugging back slightly. Unlike the other women at *Nouvelle Placage,* she hadn't dolled herself up in silk and simpering sweetness to get all cozy with a man. She had a job to do. And the longer she swayed around the bedroom with this intoxicating fed, the harder it would be for her to accomplish her goal.

"You received a scarf," he said.

"Yes, I know," she snapped. "I was there. I delivered it to your field office myself, which I didn't have to do, you know. I could have waited until I was done with this case. I should have waited."

"Maybe, but then you might be dancing with an unhinged rapist rather than with me."

He spun her, the twirl both expert and effortless.

She gasped, a little dizzy. A little impressed.

"It matched the ones left with the other victims," he explained, his voice soft, but weighted with importance. "Didn't the agent-in-charge explain what the scarf meant?"

She groaned. "He just said that some wack job who thinks he's the Frito Bandito might try and abduct me to fulfill some sort of non-sexual sex fantasy."

Agent Murrieta stiffened, but continued to maneuver her in a tight square in the center of the room. When she looked up, she was surprised to find that his eyes had hardened into twin blocks of blue ice.

"It's not non-sexual. Not anymore. He's escalated. You're in serious danger, Ms. Lécuyer. And I'm going to make sure he doesn't get to you, whether you want me to or not."

3

FRITO BANDITO? Had she just equated his storied ancestor with the retired mascot for corn chips? At the spot where his right hand rested just below her shoulder blade, his father's ring burned.

Or at least, he imagined it did.

The family heirloom had reportedly once belonged to the very man whose reputation Claire had just unknowingly insulted. Centered by an emerald etched with a Z and flanked by two large opals that reflected vibrant blues and greens among the inky black, the ring had always been his father's most treasured possession. Now it connected Michael to his brothers, to his family legacy—and to this case.

No one at the FBI knew that Michael was the direct descendant of Joaquin Murrieta, the very real and very notorious California renegade after whom the fictionalized Zorro was based. He'd drawn the line at allowing the unsub to be branded with the name associated with his famous forebear, so he certainly wasn't going to let Joaquin Murrieta be reduced to a mustachioed Mexican stereotype.

"The unknown subject, whom my colleagues have

dubbed The Bandit, is both delusional and dangerous. Just because he's fixated on a character who wore black masks and capes in the movies doesn't make him any less dangerous. Especially to a delicate woman like yourself."

The last part was a cheap shot, but it hit the target. Her eyes flashed and he had to increase the pressure of his grip to keep her swaying to the music rather than punching him in the face.

He shouldn't have baited her, but somehow, he couldn't help himself. Unintended insult to his ancestor notwithstanding, Claire Lécuyer took herself entirely too seriously. He would know. He usually did the same.

But not tonight. Not with her. Casting aside the fact that he was dressed like an idiot while prancing around for some voyeur's video camera with moves he hadn't used since his ballroom-obsessed fifth grade teacher taught her class the box step, Michael felt entirely at ease. Dancing with Claire—no, holding her close—felt nearly as natural as taking her into his protective custody.

Again, he wondered about the ring. According to legend, it allowed the wearer to access the three qualities most often associated with the dashing character the unsub had appropriated for his sexual fantasy. A strong desire to impart justice to the wicked. An insatiable desire for adventure. And, of course, an enviable talent with women.

Michael didn't believe any of that nonsense, but he knew one thing for sure: if he was going to go up against a madman to save Claire Lécuyer, he'd take all the help he could get.

"I don't need a bodyguard," she murmured, her lips drawn in a severe line. "I used to be a cop, you know."

"Of course I know," he replied, taking a chance at a second twirl that made her gasp in surprise. "I've made it my business to know everything about you. At least, everything that could be collected in an FBI file. But law enforcement experience doesn't make you invincible."

"No, but it does make me smarter about my safety than the average woman."

"So smart that I had my hand around your throat and could have taken you out of here without anyone thinking it was more than some sexual game?"

Claire swallowed, the movement mesmerizing, particularly in the uncertain lamp light. Getting the jump on her had been a lucky break, but she didn't need to know that. Between the music, the lights, the swirl and swish of multi-colored gowns, it was a miracle he'd spotted her so quickly.

Though she was pretty tough to miss.

The rest of the women had gone to great lengths to look young and fresh, but Claire was naturally both. She'd applied her makeup with a light hand and wore a gown of pale ivory that emphasized the rich caramel hue of her skin. From the curves and lines in her shoulders and bare arms, he guessed that she worked out regularly—probably outside in the wet Louisiana heat. Despite the sweet young persona she'd adopted, she moved with a bold confidence that had snatched the attention of nearly every other man in the room. Any with taste.

For that reason, he'd acted quickly. The minute he'd sensed her scanning the room for the woman she was looking for, he'd darted into action.

But for all he knew, the Bandit had been in the room, too, stalking her just like he was.

"Is that what this is?" she asked. "Some sort of sexual game you've invented to get me into bed?"

"Don't flatter yourself," he replied, trying not to give the idea any serious consideration. "This is all an act we're putting on for whoever is watching us. We'll play their game until I can get you the hell out of here."

"I'm not leaving," she insisted.

"You have a maniac after you."

Her frown emphasized her plump lips. "You don't think I'd notice if someone was stalking me?"

"No," he answered simply. "Not this guy. He knows all about you. He knows you used to be a cop and that you're now a private investigator. He'd realize that you'd be a challenge. He'd change his mode of operation. He'll pull out all the stops. Whatever it takes."

"But how could he get in here, with all the security? And how would he know I was here? I had to be super cautious to make sure these people didn't suspect I was lying to them about who I was."

"I found you. And I got in on less than a day's notice. For all you know, he owns this joint."

She snorted. "That'd be one hell of a coincidence. Your case and mine intertwining so neatly? He's not here."

Michael tugged her closer. She pulled back, trying again to twist out of his hold, but he wouldn't let her. Whoever was on the other end of that camera was likely getting a kick out of this push-pull, but Michael was losing patience. He might find her strength sexy as hell, but he wasn't going to let her run headfirst into danger.

"You don't know where he is, and neither do I," he confessed, turning her toward the camera while he spoke directly into her ear. "This man ingratiates himself into the lives of his victims long before he sends them a scarf. He learns their habits. He memorizes their routines. He doesn't have a name or a face, but he's always around.

Maybe he's the guy who delivers flowers to your neighbor. Maybe he's the new tenant in the building two doors down. Maybe he's the guy walking his dog down your street who seems more interested in his text messages than his surroundings. Trust me when I tell you he's been watching you for weeks, maybe months. If he's sent you the scarf, he already knows more about you than I do—maybe more than you know about yourself."

The song ended. Michael stumbled when she drew up short, her cheeks slightly paler than before.

She waited until the next song started before she asked, "You think he's here?"

"I don't know."

He swept her back into his arms. This time the music was slower, more sensual, more intimate, requiring not so much measured movements as close contact swaying. Michael had never been much of a dancer, but moving with her in his arms felt organic. Intoxicating.

"I need a drink," she said, pulling away.

She spun to the table beside the bed and fumbled with the crystal decanter. With her back to him, he became instantly enraptured by her long, kissable neck, slim shoulder blades and trim waist. And though her skirt adequately hid the curve of her hips and legs, he imagined that underneath the silk was a body just as smooth as the satiny material.

She was pouring generous portions of brandy into the snifters when he approached her from behind. He spared the camera in the air vent a glance. Someone was capturing their every move, their every touch.

This should have worried him.

And yet, it didn't.

"Brandy?" Claire offered.

Michael did not back away, but accepted the glass

with what he hoped was an easy smile. "I take it some people don't sign up to participate, but just to watch?"

She took a generous sip. "And here I thought you'd come here knowing everything about this place."

"There wasn't time for everything. Just enough to get me through the door."

She spun prettily, then settled herself on a corner of the bed. To the casual observer, the way she let the snifter linger just at the edge of her lips would appear seductive and coy. Michael noticed that as well. But he also recognized that she'd positioned herself so that when he stood across from her, his shoulder braced against the tall bed post, their faces weren't visible to the camera.

"And how'd you manage that, anyway?" she asked. "It costs a minimum of $10,000 for a man to buy his way in. That doesn't even count the gifts and gratuities he has to lavish on his mistress of choice. I can't imagine the FBI fronting you the money just so you can get me out of here."

"The FBI has no idea I'm here."

"Why not?" she asked.

"Wasn't time. Once I figured out where you'd gone, which, admittedly, wasn't easy, I could either follow procedure or find you before the bad guy did. I hope you agree I made the right choice."

She sipped her brandy again. He hadn't imagined her to be the thoughtful type—from what he'd read about her, she was more of an act-now, ask-questions-later type of woman. But something about him made her look before she leapt, and he wasn't sure if that was a good sign or a bad omen.

"Where'd you get the money?" she asked.

"Does it matter?"

"I'm making small talk," she said, turning her face

so that her fake smile flashed at the camera. "Trying to decide whether or not to trust you. It's not like I had a chance to examine your credentials thoroughly. I barely saw them."

"Trust me," he murmured. "Your aunt looked them over carefully. I take it you've given her some tips on ferreting out fakes?"

"Ha! Clarice taught me. She may be pushing sixty, but she's the sharpest woman I know."

"And she thought it was a good idea for you to come here when a serial psycho is after you? Oh, wait, you left out that part."

"Your FBI counterparts didn't say anything about him being a serial psycho," she pointed out. "They just said he was a stalker. And I didn't want her to be involved at all, but even I'm not hotheaded enough to come into this place alone. She has my cell phone and can dial 9-1-1 like a pro. She's also a crack shot and carries a .32 in her purse. I know my plan wasn't the best, but it's all I could come up with on short notice. Sound familiar?"

With a chuckle, he toasted her with his snifter, then took a sip of the liqueur, not at all impressed by the taste, but appreciating the fortifying heat. He and Claire did have one very big thing in common—they'd both come here on false pretenses. If either one of them was found out, they'd be in a boatload of trouble. From inside and out.

"Very familiar."

"Then why didn't you just wait for me to get home? If I'm lucky, my case will be done tonight. I saw my client's ex-wife's alias on a guest list. Once I locate her and get her signature, I'll be out of here."

"Unless her fake name is fake."

"What?"

"In the five cases we've connected to the unsub, he takes his victim within forty-eight hours of sending the scarf. You received yours the day before yesterday, right? Maybe if I hadn't shown up tonight and enticed you to this bedroom, you wouldn't be coming home. Ever."

Outside the room, someone moved. Michael turned to the door in time to see shadows dance in the transom window. Voices argued in hushed tones. Maybe his device hadn't worked as designed, or maybe the music had not been loud enough to mask their conversation.

Or perhaps, the voyeurs behind the video cameras were tired of watching them talk.

He set down his untouched brandy and grabbed Claire by the arm, tugging her close so that their lips were barely an inch apart.

She splayed her hand flat against his chest. "What do you think you're doing?"

The lock on the door behind them jiggled.

"Taking what I paid for."

CLAIRE'S SENSES EXPLODED in rapid succession. First, she heard the muffled sound of footsteps outside in the hall. Then Special Agent Murrieta had her on her feet, in his arms, his mouth on hers.

And oh, what a mouth it was.

Unlike in the ballroom, where he'd toyed between gentle and insistent, his touch from both hands and lips was now rough and unyielding. At nearly the same moment, her nostrils inhaled the spiced masculine scent of his cologne and her tongue, slightly numbed by the brandy, swelled with the powerful flavors of coffee, mint and man.

When the door burst open behind them, she did not have to feign a gasp of surprise.

He threw her behind him.

"What is the meaning of this?" he barked.

Claire leaned around his solid frame and saw the dark-skinned woman, flanked by two imposing men who matched Michael in height, but surpassed him in girth by about fifty pounds each.

The woman iced up her spine and spoke first. "I'm afraid we don't recognize you, sir. Are you on our guest list?"

Claire's mind whirled with myriad explanations, but even as she opened her mouth to speak, she realized that doing so would ruin the charade. Women of the *gens de couleur libre* were notoriously independent, but probably not so much when in the presence of their men. Even as she decided to hold her tongue, the FBI agent who'd gone to such lengths to blend into this world dug into his jacket and produced a square of thick vellum paper. An exclusive invitation to this weekend's event.

"This is an outrage," he muttered, tossing the card to the floor.

The woman did not react, but waited for one of her lackeys to retrieve the invitation and place it gingerly into her hands. The woman's black eyes assessed Special Agent Murrieta from head to toe, sparing Claire only a single, questioning glance that she answered with genuine confusion. Who did the woman think he was, anyway? And why had they burst in?

One of the goons turned off the gramophone-disguised CD player, then proceeded to examine it from all angles. If he found the amplifier, they'd both be turfed out of the place. But Michael must have hidden it well. After two tense minutes, the man turned to the woman in charge and gave a hopeless shrug.

The corners of her mouth dropped into a frown.

"My apologies, *monsieur*," she said with a little bow, her head tilted even as she gave Claire a second once-over. "It's just that this *mademoiselle* is new to our society, as well. It is…unusual…for two people uninitiated in our ways to go off together so early in the evening."

The woman's mouth drew into a straight, unyielding line, but Claire could have bet she was censoring herself like a preacher on a tirade. They hadn't been made, but the people-in-charge were suspicious.

Great. Just great.

"My arrangement with the *mademoiselle* was made in complete accordance with your guidelines," he said, snatching the invitation back. "And I may be new here, but I still prefer fresh flowers to the dry, wilted ones so heavily in attendance."

From her vantage point, Claire could not see Michael's expression, but his tone of voice tipped his metaphor into the dangerous range. He'd meant to insult the woman—and from the fury in her eyes, he'd accomplished his task.

"We will not disturb you again," she said stiffly, "but we will be watching. To ensure you enjoy your stay."

Her smile reeked of sarcasm. She spun on her heel and left, the two goons trailing behind her. The door closed and locked again—this time, from the outside.

Claire raised herself on her tip-toes so that she could whisper in her so-called rescuer's ear. "Uh-oh. Think we're in trouble?"

Michael reset the CD, ensuring that it played on a continuous loop, then turned and wrapped his hands fully around her waist. His grip, possessive and intense, sapped her breath.

"Not yet, but you heard the woman. They'll be watching us."

Claire couldn't miss the glint of anticipation in Michael's eyes or the flare of his nostrils that told her his senses were heightened—on alert. They might be in deep shit, but she suspected that the deeper the shit, the more excited this clever FBI agent became.

He fed on danger. Boy, could she ever relate.

"So what do you suggest we do?" she asked.

"Well, if they're watching," he said, giving the camera a cursory glance, "I say we should give them a show that brings down the house."

4

THE MINUTE MICHAEL pressed his mouth to Claire's again, a burning question seared through the sensations of her soft flesh against his.

Just how far was she willing to go?

And even more important…how far was he?

He had not planned to kiss her. Beyond working his way into *Nouvelle Placage,* he had not planned much of anything. The more he'd learned about the plantation party, the more he figured he would have to flirt and be charming before he convinced her that her personal safety was more important than finding some woman who'd willfully abandoned her kids.

But now they were trapped. He could flash his badge and get them out, but that would blow her case, and possibly his, too. Telling her the Bandit could be here watching had not just been a scare tactic. In all his other attacks, the guy had stalked his victims for weeks and ended up knowing more about their lives than anyone had imagined. If he was here watching Claire and realized she was being protected by the FBI, he could run.

And then he could change his patterns. If he did that, they might never get this close to finding him—not until he'd hurt another string of women. And maybe this time, he wouldn't stop at kidnapping or rape. If Michael and Claire utterly destroyed The Bandit's sick fantasy, he might cross the line and kill.

They were in now—they had to play this through to the end.

Wasn't like it was a huge sacrifice to kiss Claire Lécuyer senseless anyway.

Since joining the Bureau right out of college, he'd trussed himself to his job. What free time he had, he'd given to his family, with only short, uninspired relationships that fired up quick and burned out fast. Never in his life had he kissed a woman he knew he shouldn't— with strangers watching every slide of his hand down her waist, every curve of his fingers through the folds of her dress.

It was exciting.

It was dangerous. One call to his superiors, one viral video linked to the Bureau could destroy everything he'd worked for.

So why couldn't he let her go?

Her lips were soft and slick; her tongue was hot and insistent. With no hesitation, no boundaries, she explored the full breadth of his mouth, skimming across his teeth and igniting a flame deep in his gut that would be impossible to extinguish, even if everyone in the plantation house burst in and doused him with pails of ice cold water.

Scrunching up the voluminous skirt in his hands, he found the back of her thighs, bare between her stockings and some sort of cottony drawers that cradled her backside like a cloud. Her flesh prickled and he wanted to warm her. Create friction. Share the burn.

She broke her mouth away from his, then trailed her

lips over his jawline. "Is this what they train you for at Quantico?"

He braced his hands on the crest of her buttocks, re-sisting the urge to lift her fully and completely against his erection. "Not last time I checked."

She followed her path of feather light kisses with a lush swipe of her tongue, her long lashes hiding her gaze as it trained on the camera. "You must really want my cooperation if you're willing to put your credentials on the line for a chance to feel me up. My ass is choice, but probably not worth your career."

Michael laughed, the sound bursting from his chest like the stopper on a bottle of sparkling wine. Self-deprecating, she was not. She was, however, gorgeous, sexy, sensual and irresistible. From the first moment he'd laid eyes on her, his need to touch her, taste her, seduce her had been harder and harder to fight.

And this wasn't like him.

Not like him at all.

As if on cue, the center emerald of the Murrieta ring caught a flash of lamplight.

Up until a month ago, Michael had been exactly like his oldest brother, Alejandro. Serious. Responsible. Con-cerned with expectations and appearances and all the other prison bars society erected to keep anarchy at bay.

But then Alex had taken possession of their de-ceased father's ring. In the span of a week, his entire life had changed. Not only had he fallen in love with a woman who'd completely lied to him about who she was, but he'd invested a large amount of cash and clout to ensure that Daniel, their middle brother, got off on the trumped-up charges that could have meant a long stint in the state penitentiary.

Now, Michael had the ring. Was it a coincidence that

he was willing to turn away from what was right in order to revel in something wicked and wanton and undeniably wrong?

"Ordinarily, I'm a by-the-book kind of guy," he said, dipping his head so that he could run his tongue down the elegant curve of her bare neck. "But for this case, I might have to push some limits."

She arched her back, and with no reason not to, he smoothed his hungry lips across her collar bone and then down the edge of her square-cut bodice. "Personally or professionally?"

He didn't know the answer. He wasn't sure he wanted to. The instinct to remain in the moment, grab what he could while it lasted, proved more powerful than anything he'd ever felt before. He realized he'd say just about anything to taste the skin between her shoulder and neck.

"It's all about the case," he said.

"Which? Mine or yours?"

"Does it matter?"

"It does to me."

She braced her hands on his shoulders and gave a push that instantly disengaged his mouth from her flesh. "I have less than three days to find the woman I'm looking for. The only lead I have is that she's here, for this weekend only. I won't hide in this room with you and I won't run away on the off chance this so-called Bandit of yours has somehow managed to follow me here. Not until I've done what my client has paid me to do."

The determination in her voice doused his libido.

"This man has targeted you, Claire. He won't stop until he gets you."

Her light laugh sparked a trail of heat underneath his skin, as if someone had injected his blood cells with gun powder and her confident smirk had lit the fuse.

"He's never gone up against anyone like me before."

This much was true. However, her cocky strength could just be the stressor that sent the Bandit over the edge.

He clutched her arms and forced her back a few inches, which, unfortunately, did nothing to squelch his need to kiss her again.

"Maybe not, but he's still a serious threat."

"He hasn't killed anyone."

"No, but he's assaulted and raped. It's only a matter of time before he goes even further, Claire. And maybe you're the one he's been working his way up to murder."

He watched fear skitter across her expression—which impressed him. It was one thing to be confident, but it was something else to think you were invincible. Something incredibly unwise, if not downright stupid.

And Claire Lécuyer did not strike him as stupid.

"Why me?" she questioned. "Don't criminals usually follow the path of least resistance?"

"Not always and not in this case. I fully intend to brief you on why he sought you out, but not here. This isn't a game, Claire."

She nodded, her mouth pursed in a serious, contemplative scrunch. After a moment, she locked her stare with his. "But I'm the best chance you have to catch him, right?"

His stomach constricted. She wasn't going to give up easily.

"This is the first time we've had any knowledge of who he's after before he's attacked."

Her increasingly confident grin bloomed into a full-on smile. "Then you need me to cooperate, Agent Murrieta. And for that, you will have to help me solve my case."

So it had come to this: blackmail. Or if he was feeling generous, *quid pro quo*. He strolled to the bedside table to put down his brandy, giving him time to think. He'd had two things on his mind when he'd broken the rules in coming here. First, he would protect Claire by getting her out as soon as possible. Then, from a safe location, he would determine a way to use the knowledge they had about the Bandit's patterns to set a trap and catch him. Except for the pull of desire that had caught him unaware, nothing had changed. He still had two goals.

Protect Claire and catch a kidnapper.

In that order.

If he delayed his plans a couple of hours to give her what she wanted, who would it harm? The Bandit would not get to her here. He'd make sure of that.

"Before we negotiate, you need to know the whole story. This unsub isn't your ordinary wack job. According to a profile provided by the Behavioral Analysis Unit at Quantico, he's a fast-evolving, highly intelligent, power-reassurance rapist who believes he's the reincarnation of the famous masked bandit from colonial California, righting wrongs during the daytime and seducing beautiful women in the dead of night."

"Seducing? Don't you mean drugging and kidnapping and tormenting?"

"To him, he's playing out this grand romance. He's not sloppy or random. He's purposeful, calculating. Patient. If he's taken the step of sending you the scarf, I'd bet money he knows you're here. He might have followed you or he might even have been the one to manipulate you into coming in the first place."

Her hand flattened against her stomach, as if the thought sickened her. "Wait, you think he hired me?

Lied about my case so that I'd come to the plantation tonight?"

Michael ran his hand down the length of her arm. Her skin was pebbled again, but this time with fear instead of desire. "Is it a coincidence that your great-grandmother on your mother's side was black, so that you're mixed race just like the women bartered for in the real *placage* system?"

Her eyes widened. "How did you know that?"

"It's my job to know, Claire. The more I know, the better I can protect you. And if I know it, you can bet he knows. Your family has been in New Orleans for centuries. One of your ancestors might have taken part in the real quadroon balls. Maybe in his obsession with you, he found that out and came up with a plan to lure you here. Or maybe it's just a coincidence. They do happen sometimes. He's never gone to so much trouble before, but maybe he's never had to. He's evolving. And like you said, you're a different kind of victim."

She straightened her shoulders. "I'm not anyone's victim."

"Not yet," he replied. "And if you cooperate with me, not ever. But how sure are you of your client? Did you meet with him? Did you have adequate time to check out his story?"

He watched her throat bob as she swallowed, watched her eyes narrow first with doubt, then with shock and finally with fury. When she jumped to her feet, ostensibly to object to him questioning her professionalism, he pulled her into his arms and kissed her into silence.

She struggled to get free, but he did not yield. If the unsub was in the building, the safest place for her to be while they worked out a strategy was this bedroom. No device was going to cover up the sound of her shouting.

"Let me go," she insisted, her words muffled by his mouth.

"Don't struggle," he murmured back. "They're still watching. For all we know, he's watching."

He released her arms, but she remained flush against him, her gaze locked with his. In that moment, he couldn't resist drowning himself in the creamy jade of her eyes, in the sweet milk and toasted coffee shade of her skin.

She was stunning. Not run of the mill tanned-and-gorgeous like he saw every day in California, but instead, everything the sponsors of *Nouvelle Placage* promised. Like the women bartered for hundreds of years ago, Claire was exotic, erotic and fresh in a way that had nothing to do with innocence and everything to do with attitude.

"You really think he set me up?" she whispered.

To her credit, she regained her calm quickly.

"I don't know," he said. "But to beat this guy, we've got to be smarter than he is. And we have to stick together. One contingency he hasn't planned for is you having someone to watch your back. Or other parts of you, as the case may be."

He'd crossed the line again, but he couldn't help himself, particularly when her lips quirked into a tiny smile. She was so gorgeous, so defiant, so unlike any woman he'd been this close to.

As much as he cared about this case—as much as he cared about keeping her safe and ensuring the legacy of his family name—he cared about her more.

At least, he cared about kissing her, touching her, tasting her.

With focused fascination, he watched her coil her finger within one of the springy curls dangling beside her cheek. If not for the music still playing beside them and the rapid pounding of blood surging through his veins, Michael might have heard her brain processing all the information he'd just shared.

Her gaze darted to the camera hidden behind the air vent, to the shadows mingling with the light beaming from under the door, to the brandy, and then, back to him.

Of all the variables she'd considered, she assessed him with the keenest deliberation. She stepped back a few inches, looking him up and down with her eyes narrowed, her tongue tracing a hungry path between her plump, pink lips.

In an instant, their roles were reversed. He was no longer the monied Southern gentleman considering his options as he strolled through the lines of lovely ladies waiting downstairs.

He was the one on the block.

And she didn't look at him like a sweet, innocent ingénue. The glint in her impossibly opaque green eyes was that of a distinctively modern woman, one who knew the pleasures that could be found in the arms of the right man.

With a squeal that announced she was back in character, she grabbed his hands and dragged him behind the silk screen in the corner. To anyone listening at the door, her giggles reverberated with giddy excitement. He barely had time to lock his brain on what was happening when she started to tear at his cravat.

"They can still see us from behind this screen," she said, making short work of the loose knot at his neck. "Our shadows, at the very least. We're going to have to make this look good."

Despite the rush of blood roaring through his ears,

Michael pieced together her meaning. She still assumed his kisses and innuendos were part of his cover—part of some plan to convince the gatekeepers of *Nouvelle Placage* that the two of them were just like everyone else in attendance—horny, costumed fetishists who'd come here not to dig into their secret world, but to revel in forbidden desires.

Okay. He could work with that. Especially if it meant stripping down with Claire and discovering the true lusciousness beneath her elaborate gown.

He spun her around and loosened the ties on her bodice.

"Just how far are you willing to take this?" he asked, trailing his tongue from the base of her skull, down her spine, to the gradually spreading laces of her gown.

"As far as we have to," she said, breathless, her voice hitching when his tongue hit the spot directly between her shoulder blades.

She tasted like a gourmet dessert, a combination of flavors that played with the notions of salty and sweet.

"You?" she asked, tossing a sassy glance over her shoulder.

In another time, another place, another situation, he might have said that he'd only go as far as necessary to keep the mission intact. But here, now, with Claire, under the influence of his ancestor's ring, all bets were off.

"As far as you want to go," he replied.

She spun around. With her top sufficiently loosened, the stiff material of the bodice and sleeves floated around her corseted breasts like clouds of shimmering satin. Michael's mouth instantly watered for a taste.

Just one taste.

"Care to be more specific?" she asked.

He smoothed his hands down her back, his fingers spanning her slim waist. Claire was not willowy or thin, but curvaceous and athletic. Her arms were tanned and muscled, but she possessed a natural softness that made him lift her up from her elbows so he could properly inhale the scent of the lotions clinging to her skin.

"How specific?"

He pressed her full against his body, so that she could not mistake the feel of his erection even through the layers of her gown.

"Oh."

The sound of her surprise, coupled with the flush of pink across her cheeks, fired him even more. He tugged her to him, his lips so close to hers he could feel her breath as he spoke.

"I came here with no intention beyond getting you to safety as soon as possible. But I'd be lying if I denied how beautiful you are or how hot you look in that dress, especially now that it's half off. Making love to you would not be a hardship. In fact, it would be my pleasure."

Her mouth dropped open momentarily, but then she laughed. She wrapped her arms around his neck and pierced him with a stare so bold, he thought he might lose his mind.

"Then I think I'm going to like working with you, Special Agent Murrieta."

"If we do it right, it won't be work. And please, call me Michael."

"By all means, Michael. Let's give those bastards behind the camera something worth watching."

5

"WHERE THE HELL are you, Michael?"

Special Agent Ruby Dawson muttered the question under her breath, her eyes trained on the blank screen of her cell phone. Except for one cryptic message telling her that Claire Lécuyer had taken off and that Michael was following a lead to catch up with her, all Ruby knew about her partner's whereabouts was that he'd gone undercover without backup. If anything happened to him because he couldn't wait six hours until she arrived on a later flight from San Francisco, she was going to kill him.

"May I buy you another?"

Ruby glanced up, momentarily surprised to discover a fine-looking man in a pale guayabera and khaki shorts smiling at her. He was holding a sweating mug of beer, nearly as empty as hers. His blond hair was cropped short. His cheeks were rough from several days of not shaving and his eyes, an arresting mixture of browns from deep chocolate to rich gold, shone with the kind of hopefulness only experienced by a man on vacation who'd just spotted a single chick in a bar.

Really? Now? Tonight?

Inwardly, Ruby groaned. Any other time, she might have grinned provocatively and enjoyed the free drink while she sized up the guy, doing a mini-profile in her head that would determine whether she said yes to his inevitable invitation to dance or declined when he offered to drive her home. Especially here, in Draper's Dive, a cheesy, nautical-themed bar she'd been hanging out in since she was eighteen and her mom had taken an apartment two blocks over from. She'd honed her people-watching skills here, determining the winners and losers with such accuracy that the former owner had suggested she get a job with the FBI.

She'd taken his advice, and every time she came back to town, she hit the old place to drink a beer in his honor.

Didn't happen very often anymore, but it was a tradition, much as it was a given that at some point during her tribute drink, a guy was going to make a pass.

Under other circumstances, she would not have minded. She was pushing forty, single, and lately, a little undersexed. But Michael was out of touch, and no matter how cold and delicious the local brew felt against the back of her throat, she had to track him down. She didn't have time for a real diversion—even one with lips curved into a casual, if not arresting, smile.

"I can buy my own, thanks," she said, turning her attention back to her cell phone, ignoring the twinge of sensation in her nipples.

That's how it always started—with a zing. Followed by full-out flirting, laughing, usually a little more drinking and, if she was lucky, a succession of dance moves that would coat her skin with a slick sheen of sweat and inspire her to peel away her clothing, one layer at a time.

Where it usually ended, if she wasn't on the job, was in bed. But this time, she hadn't come home to New

Orleans for fun. She was here to work…although, with
Michael running around half-cocked and out of com-
munication range, she really didn't have anything to do.

"Of course you could buy your own," the man said,
sidling in between her bar stool and the empty one beside
her, but making no move to sit. "But why would you if
I'm offering?"

His bold self-confidence was interesting. He was
good looking, even if in a little too familiar "movie star"
way. The vibe he threw off wasn't over-the-top pushy or
creepy.

Just…persistent.

And Ruby kind of liked persistent.

"I don't know you," she replied, turning her shoulder
so he'd get the hint.

He laughed. "I've only been in town for a few days.
I don't know anyone." He leaned around her and held
out his hand. "David Brandon."

She sighed. She hadn't traveled across the United
States to flirt with some tourist in a French Quarter bar.
However, what she had come here to do—provide Michael with backup while they tracked down the Bandit—
was on hold until her partner resurfaced.

As soon as she'd secured her rental car from the airport, she'd verified that the Bandit's likeliest next victim,
Claire Lécuyer, was not home; and from the way the
place was locked up tight, she wasn't coming back anytime soon. Ruby had then checked in with the local FBI
office and learned that while Michael had alerted their
counterparts to his arrival, he'd given them no intel re-
garding his plans.

He had asked for the name and location of a discreet
costume shop, though. That made her scalp itch with
anxiety. Ever since Michael's brother had given him their

father's ring, Michael had been different. He'd always been laser-focused on the job, but with his discovery of his new brothers—the heretofore unknown older brother, Alejandro, and the recently released jailbird, Danny— his drive and determination had hit new highs. Why couldn't he have waited a few hours for her to show up? Instead, he'd gone off on his own, and until she found what the hell he was up to, she had nothing but time on her hands.

She gave the guy a little half-smile and said, "I'm Ruby," keeping her last name to herself.

Mr. Handsome gestured to her pilsner glass. "May I?"

She shrugged and he took her nonchalance as acceptance. He motioned to the bartender to bring fresh drinks and then turned his assessing eyes to hers.

"You look comfortable," he said. "You live around here?"

Her half-smile blossomed into a full grin. He was good. He turned the standard "where are you from?" into an interesting—and accurate—observation.

"Used to," she replied.

"Lucky," he said. "I'd move here in a heartbeat if I didn't have obligations elsewhere."

"Really?" she asked, skeptically. She often heard tourists make such claims, but few ever followed through. People didn't move to New Orleans on purpose. They were either born and bred here or came here to work— and there wasn't too much of that going since Katrina.

Her doubtful look did not deter him. "The food. The music. The color. The vibe. It's old and smelly, but new and exciting at the same time. You never know what's going to happen. You never know who you're going to meet."

Nice segue. Somehow, he kept the conversation about her hometown centered on her. He was good, this David Brandon.

"It's a passable party town."

"To the casual observer," he said.

"Isn't that what you are?"

He pressed his lips together, as if he withheld a secret that would fully explain his fascination with the Crescent City. "Sure, I guess. So, do you have family here?"

"Some," she answered honestly, not disturbed by his quick focus on learning more about her. It was a natural question and this guy was nothing if not natural. "A bunch stayed in Houston after Katrina 'cause they found work. My mother's people went back to Mississippi, where they were from originally, but my father's cousins and my brother toughed it out in Metarie."

The bartender arrived with the cold drafts while David expanded his questions about her family and shared a little bit about himself. She learned he had two brothers, neither of whom he knew very well, and that he'd never lived in one place very long during his childhood on account of his now-deceased mother's wandering spirit.

For her part, Ruby answered his questions with practiced care, never revealing anything important while creating the illusion that she was spilling her life's story. Some of what she said wasn't even true—her brother in Metarie was actually in a cemetery—but she'd told the lies often enough that she no longer worried about not getting the story straight.

"So if you're not in town to play," he surmised once she declined his offer for a third refill, "why come at all?"

"Work," she answered.

"What do you do?"

She speared him with an intense look and wondered whether to be honest or deflect the question.

She glanced at the clock on her cell phone. Nearly forty-five minutes had passed since David Brandon had made his first move. Michael still had not checked in and she was starting to feel the ache of cross-country travel in heavy eyelids and tight muscles around her neck.

"Law enforcement."

"No shit? Me, too."

She'd expected the guy to go running—learning that the lady was a cop often had that effect on men, especially tourists hanging out in bars and looking for a good time. But David just slid forward, and when the bartender appeared with two fresh glasses of beer that she couldn't remember him ordering, he requested a pound of steamed oysters and asked Ruby if there was anything else on the menu she'd like to share.

She declined, but couldn't fault the guy for perseverance. However, if he was trying to go the "aphrodisiac" route, he was going to be sorely disappointed. He was cute, but she wasn't in the mood. Michael should have checked in by now.

"Look, you're a nice guy, but I really need to get going."

"Before the oysters? Come on, I love some slimy crustaceans, but I can't down a whole dozen on my own. Not after all the jambalaya I had at lunch."

He patted his stomach, which looked perfectly flat to her.

It nearly hurt for her to say, "I'm sorry, but I'm not interested."

"In oysters?"

"No, I don't normally turn down the oysters here.

Their cocktail sauce is the kind you want to scoop up with a spoon. I'm just not interested in—" She waved her hand between them. "This."

He bowed his head respectfully. "That's cool. Then just stay for the oysters. I don't force my attentions on women, but when I make an offer to share a meal, I don't take it back. That wouldn't be gentlemanly, now, would it?"

Ruby rewarded his honesty by not climbing off the barstool and heading out the door. She was such a sucker for charming guys. She wasn't going to change her mind about only sharing an appetizer with him before she took off, but she didn't need to be rude, either. Even if he wasn't her type.

Yeah, he was good-looking, but scruffier than she normally preferred. And he was in law enforcement. She had a strict and unalterable policy against dating guys who shared her profession. Still, there was something in his eyes that made her want to trust him, at least long enough to finish her beer and slurp down a few steamed oysters.

"No, it wouldn't." Ruby settled into her seat and arranged her phone so she wouldn't miss the alerts if a text message or phone call came through. Maybe more chitchat would take her mind off Michael and stem the persistent feeling that even though he'd been here for only a few hours more than she had, he was already in over his head.

"So," she said, determined to stop worrying about Michael when there was nothing she could do. "What brings a cop from another jurisdiction to New Orleans?"

"Vacation, pure and simple," David answered easily. "I work in a mid-sized town in Illinois that you've never heard of and I needed a change of scenery. Heard it was best to visit New Orleans in the fall, so I came down, did some gambling, heard some real jazz, ate way more than I should have. And yet—"

His eyes lit up as the oysters arrived. He handed Ruby a small plate, a stack of napkins and a tiny fork with a lemon impaled on the end.

She removed the lemon and put it on the side. She liked lemon on raw oysters, but preferred the steamed ones with loads of the Dive's horseradish-heavy cocktail sauce. The recipe hadn't changed with the ownership, judging by the way her eyes watered when she took a sniff.

"When are you heading home?"

"Soon," he said. "I have one more thing to do before I go back."

"And what's that?" she asked.

He doused his oyster with hot sauce, then sucked it down and chased the spicy seafood with a long draft of beer.

She raised her eyebrows, waiting for him to answer. She wasn't sure why she was so curious, but the longer he avoided giving her a straight answer, the more the guy struck her as…familiar?

She was fairly certain she'd never seen him before. She had a better-than-most memory for faces, honed by studying pictures of suspects before heading out into the field to track them down. And she'd definitely never heard his voice with its distinctive Midwestern inflection. But there was something about David Brandon that made her think he'd make a fine drinking buddy on the nights when a date was hard to come by.

Just like Michael.

He finished his third oyster and finally replied, "Let's

just say that I've got a little more left of the city to see and leave it at that."

"Fair enough," she concluded, taking another oyster off the platter and this time dipping it in a small plastic tub of drawn butter.

David Brandon could keep his secrets. Her whole life, she'd been a sucker for a good mystery. And the more oysters she ate and beer she drank, the less she worried about the unsolved mystery she had no means to solve. Just where was her partner and what the hell was he doing?

IS HE WATCHING?

The thought, so illicit, so disturbing, dove with determination through the waves of pleasure washing through Claire's body as Special Agent Michael Murrieta, the man charged with keeping her safe from a crazed kidnapper, suckled the pulse point on her neck. She should care that a man who had targeted her as his next victim might be on the other side of that hidden camera. She should be creeped out that some sicko would get off on watching her fall under the sensual spell of another man—or worse, that the sight was infuriating him to the point that he planned all manner of punishments for her once he finally had her in his possession.

But that was the problem, wasn't it? She knew the guy was never going to get his hands on her. Not if she had anything to say about it, which she did. And not with Michael Murrieta standing in his way.

That the FBI agent had caught her unaware downstairs had wounded her pride. It had also upped her confidence in his skills to a trust level she hadn't experienced since she'd been a rookie cop and thought every veteran would jump into the line of fire to protect one of their own.

Boy, had she learned differently.

Michael, on the other hand, had quickly earned her respect, not with his leather bound credentials, but with the cunning means he'd used to inject himself into her investigation. He hadn't thumped his chest and demanded she put her job aside for the benefit of his case. He'd blended seamlessly into this world and paid just as much attention to keeping his investigation intact as he had to hers.

And the way he was tracing a sensuous path from her neck to her ear with his tender kisses wasn't hurting.

She knew he was breaking all kinds of protocols by involving himself with her, and the realization intensified the pleasure of his body against hers. With every swipe of his lips over her skin, every graze of his hands over her flesh, he proved what he was made of. It was one thing to don a crazy costume and go undercover long enough to find her, but it was entirely something else to play out a very real, very effective seduction of the woman he needed for his case.

His superiors would not be happy if the tape leaked out. She had no idea how the politics of the FBI worked, but if it was anything like her time with the New Orleans Police Department, he was in for some serious shit hitting the fans. She'd lost her job just because she'd put justice ahead of the chain of command.

God help him, but nothing turned her on more than a man willing to buck the system in order to get what he wanted—a fact made all the more exciting when what he wanted was her.

"Since we're relative strangers," he whispered between swipes of his tongue along the shell of her ear, "you're going to have to tell me what you like. You know. To make this believable."

The underlying chuckle in his voice told her he'd added that last part to tease her.

"Is that all you're interested in?" she asked. "Making this believable for the pervs on the other side of the camera?"

He slid his hands down the arch of her back and cupped her butt with hungry possessiveness. "What do you think?"

She responded by tearing her hands through his hair, which was soft and scented with tangy citrus. "I think you're hot for me."

"I think you're as smart as your file says you are."

"Then how are you going to stop yourself from taking more than I might be willing to offer?" She slipped her hands between the open sides of his shirt and spread the material so that her palms rested on his broad, muscled shoulders. "You're obviously very strong. And big."

The corner of his mouth quirked up in a grin that melted her insides to a liquid heat. Drop by drop, the slick moisture eased through her body, then soothed the gentle throbbing between her thighs.

"Unlike the guy I'm protecting you from, I don't have to use force to get what I want."

"No, you're using your case."

"So are you," he countered.

She placed a kiss on his pec, swirling her tongue and loving the salted flavor of his skin. "True. It's going to be really, really *hard* not to go all the way. Guy like you. Girl like me."

He grabbed the sleeves of her dress and slowly, sensually, tugged the material off her shoulders. She was suddenly very glad her aunt had convinced her to wear a corset so that she was not completely bared as the dress caught around her waist. In fact, she was better than bared. She was laced-in and pushed up in the most delicious manner, judging by the fire that ignited in his eyes.

"In situations like this," he said, "I find that *hard* is a good state to be in."

He brushed a trail of kisses across her chest, sparking an electric charge through the tips of her nipples. When he traced his fingers down the crisscrossed laces at her spine, she wondered…no, she *wished*…that he'd latch on to the satin ribbon that held the damned thing together, tug hard and set her body free.

No matter the banter between them, Claire knew this wasn't just an act for the camera—not for him and definitely not for her. She wasn't shy about sex. She liked it. She also hadn't had any in a good long while, a fact she hadn't been entirely aware of until now.

When had she stopped caring about sex? When had she stopped looking for the occasional lover to scratch her itch and give her a reason to leave the house for something other than work?

Now she had a chance not only to enjoy the rare, sensual delights of a man who knew how to use his body—and better, how to use hers—but also to keep her latest case from falling apart.

It was a win-win. She'd entered this old plantation house fully aware that the people around her had come here for sex, but she'd never planned to join them.

And yet, here she was, wishing that Special Agent Murietta would stop coiling the ribbons holding her corset together around his finger and just yank the knot free already.

"Laissez les bons temps rouler," she murmured, lifting

Michael's face so that she could smooth her cheek against his.

"Excuse me?"

"It's what we say here in the Big Easy. *Let the good times roll.*"

He arched a brow, emphasizing the surprise in his eyes, dark from the expansion of his pupils.

"Is that an invitation?" he asked.

"Do you need an invitation? I could use the backside of that vellum card to write one."

But he clearly needed nothing more than her consent, because with a growl, he tugged her lingerie loose. When she breathed out a sigh of relief, the stays surrendered and the corset slipped a half inch down her torso, baring her nipples to his widening eyes.

His throat bobbed with his deep swallow and Claire's body thrummed with anticipation. When he licked his lips, she nearly groaned. He splayed his hands on her back, forcing her to arch upward so he could feast on her with his eyes—a feast that heightened her own hunger to a ravenous level.

He wanted her. She wanted him. So they'd take. That's how things had rolled in New Orleans since the first French fur trappers had settled the bayous. Total surrender to lusty urges was a time-honored tradition. And who was she to argue with tradition?

She ripped the rest of Michael's shirt aside and her hands spanned across his chest, tweaking his pale nipples, mimicking the attention she desperately wanted from him. She flicked her tongue across his flesh and suckled lightly while her hands dropped down his tapered torso to the rigid erection she could feel through his loose-cut pants.

If the so-called unsub was watching, then she hoped

he learned a lesson. Claire Lécuyer didn't get off on guys who resorted to drugs and masks and one-sided fake seductions. She wanted a man like Michael—hot, smart and honest. A man willing to risk everything just to have her, even if it was a make out session behind a screen.

"I'll tell you something," she said, her words coming out in ragged breaths while his nimble fingers worked at the last ties of her dress. At last the satin dropped to the floor, leaving her in nothing but the slack corset, bloomers, stockings and kitten-heeled slippers. She wasn't exactly wrapped up in Victoria's Secret lingerie, but judging by the darkening of his eyes, the outfit worked the same magic.

"By all means," he replied, his voice ragged, his gaze roaming every inch of her, as if he couldn't decide which part to sample first.

"I don't usually strip down in front of strangers."

He grinned. "I don't usually strip down with women I'm supposed to be protecting."

"Oddly enough," she said, locking stares with him as she began working the buttons of his slacks, "I believe you."

"Why is that odd?"

She slipped her fingers past the waistband of his shorts so she could squeeze his rock hard glutes.

"I don't trust easily," she said. "And sex requires trust."

He cupped her elbows, disengaging her hands and drawing them to his lips. He kissed each knuckle, taking his time, swiping his tongue into the folds between her fingers and sucking the tips with such gentle pressure that she thought her whole body might explode. She wanted that suction on her breasts, her belly, and below.

"You can trust me," he assured her, though in the miasma of need curling around her, she wasn't sure why he was still talking and not tasting. "I never break rules, but if I'm going to put my career on the line, I'm going to make sure it counts."

His words caught her up short and she forced her eyes open. "Why risk so much?"

"I can't seem to help myself," he confessed before pressing her forward so he could nibble on her shoulder. "And that's new."

As her bare nipples scraped against his chest hair, she laughed again. Delight at the sensations, at the freedom, at the irony of the situation spilled from a place deep down—a place that was simmering to be satisfied.

"I'm forever doing things I know I shouldn't," she confessed.

"And is this one of those times?" he asked, his mouth trailing closer and closer to where she desperately wanted him.

"God, I hope so."

6

MICHAEL RAN HIS hand down Claire's thigh, losing himself in the softness of her skin before he was blocked by the silky edge of her stockings. He slipped a finger beneath the snappy garter and wondered if he'd lost his mind. He was *this close* to losing his career.

But damn, what a way to go.

Somewhere in the now fogged edges of his brain, he understood that touching Claire, kissing her, arousing her was all supposed to be an act intended to convince the voyeurs on the other side of the camera that both of them had truly bought into the theme weekend. But lying to freaks who'd rather watch than do was a hell of a lot easier than lying to himself.

This had never, ever been about his case.

Or hers.

From the first minute he'd seen her downstairs, his attraction to Claire was instantaneous and undeniable. Truth be told, reading her file, which had included pictures, had implanted ideas in his brain that he had no business entertaining. She was everything he'd never sought out in a woman—strong-willed, rebellious and entirely focused on her job. During her brief stint as a

New Orleans city cop, she'd defied so many orders that her list of reprimands, transfers and punishments looked more like the rap sheet of a career criminal than the service record of a devoted law enforcement officer.

Even as a P.I., she'd broken a lot of unspoken rules, though she'd managed—barely—to stay on the right side of the law. Her reputation as a crusader willing to defy the cops in order to help her clients find justice should have made him dislike and distrust her.

Instead, she'd snared his interest like a skilled hunter with a steel trap. What made a woman like her tick? What possessed her to devote her life to rooting out criminals at the expense of the respect of her former colleagues?

But at the moment, none of that mattered. Who she'd been before they'd slipped behind the screen meant nothing to him. Beneath his touch, she became a willing, sensual woman who fired his blood and whose whimpers drove him mad.

He slid his palms slowly to her knee, reveling in the feel of the warm softness of her skin. Moisture built behind the joint, and his hand nearly slipped when he lifted her leg so that her center hit the sweet spot of his erection.

She moaned. And God help him, so did he.

The pressure was exquisite, torturous and inadequate to quell the ache of wanting. Even as he rolled his wet tongue over her nipples and caught the sound of her gasp, followed by a low, growling groan that transformed his blood cells into sharp star-shapes that pricked their way through his veins, his mouth dried. When she wrapped her leg around his waist and pressed even closer, he thought he might explode.

Her nipple was small, but stiff and responsive. With

each flick of his tongue, he could feel her pleasure building, her need growing. She grabbed his cheeks and curved her back so that he could not stop, even if he wanted to.

And he did not want to.

Instead, he slid a hand around to her buttocks and squeezed past her bloomers to the supple flesh underneath.

"Yes, yes," she crooned.

He growled against her skin, wanting more. So much more. He moved to her other breast, sucking the nipple in deep and then releasing it with his puckered lips, millimeter by millimeter until she shivered. He plucked and pleasured until she squirmed in his arms, her pelvis grinding in to his until need built to dangerous levels. Blood thundered in his ears. She was dressed up in clothes that did not match who she was, in a world that embraced neither of them, yet he could easily imagine he'd known her for years.

"Claire, beautiful Claire," he said, tickling his fingers down the curves of her ass, following a heated path to her hot core.

He clasped her buttocks, lifting her high so that he could press his mouth to the center of her ribcage. He murmured her name again, this time against her skin. He slid her down the length of his body, said, "Claire," once more before brushing his lips against hers.

She did not move except to lock her arms around him. Then, for what seemed like ages, the only parts of their bodies that moved or touched were lips, teeth and tongue. As much as he ached to press into her again, as much as he yearned to retrace the heated path to her sex, he concentrated only on the kiss.

They learned each other's flavors. They luxuriated in each other's textures and feasted on their tastes.

Without friction, Michael's body tensed and ached as if hit by a stun gun. If he denied the need to ravish her for much longer, he feared he might start to spasm or pass out. A statue of tangled nerve endings, he was keenly aware of the nearly imperceptible rise and fall of her breasts.

"Claire," he begged.

The last repetition of her name sparked a mad dash of movement. She pulled herself flush against him and deepened the kiss until her tongue crashed with his in a wild exploration. In seconds, he tore off her corset, ripped aside the voluminous bloomers and pressed her hard against the nearest flat surface, which happened to be the wall behind the screen.

His trousers dropped to the floor, nearly tripping him up around the ankles. While he'd been divesting her of her clothing, clearly, she'd done the same to him.

When she spoke, she was panting.

"Seems like a shame to waste such an impressive erection."

She squeezed her hand through the slit in his boxers and boldly grasped his sex. Michael's brain function scattered as she teased the head of his penis with the tip of her thumb, her touch light, but precise. Insistent.

Erotic.

"You're sure?" he asked, desperate for her to say yes, even if it meant tearing himself apart if she opted for no.

"God, yes," she said. She freed him from his boxers and positioned him between her legs. One slow slide, one unbridled thrust, and they'd be joined.

Voices rose in the hallway—angry female voices that

could not be drowned out by the music or the madness of their lust.

He heard the woman who'd questioned his invitation. And…

"Aunt Clarice!"

Claire pushed out from underneath him. He braced his hands to keep from crashing into the wall, then swiveled to see her sweeping her clothes up from the floor and diving into her gown, undergarments forgotten. While he scrambled to pull up his pants and thrust his hands into the sleeves of his shirt, she tugged at the lock and banged on the door.

"Maman!" she cried, her terror convincing even as she cursed a very modern blue-streak under her breath.

Michael shot forward, ready to tear the door off the hinges, but he heard the key on the other side and pulled Claire back just as it opened.

For a second, silence exploded. The dark-skinned woman who'd questioned Michael's invitation looked as if she wanted to throttle them all. Aunt Clarice waved a lace fan and gulped air, her eyes conveying some message to Claire that he could not understand.

"What's happened?" Claire asked.

Aunt Clarice gathered her calm, then turned to the woman who'd locked them inside, her shoulders back and squared.

"This is a family matter," she said.

"You can't just go bursting into rooms!" the woman argued. "There are rules. Protocols. Promises of anonymity and safety to our participants."

Claire guffawed, then hooked her thumb toward the air vent and the not-so-clandestine camera. "Sell that line to someone else, sister. If my *maman* needs to talk to me, then you can clear the hell out."

With a huff, the woman spun on her heel and marched out of the room, her goons behind her. Claire was, after all, a guest at this shin-dig, not a captive. The minute the door was closed and dead bolted—from the inside— she shuffled her aunt back toward the screen. Once they were behind it, the older woman set to putting Claire's clothing back together while chattering in a hushed tone about how she'd had to battle her way past three men in order to figure out what room they were in.

Michael made good use of the time, buttoning his pants over his persistent erection, tossing his coat over his rumpled shirt and retying his cravat, a task he failed at miserably. Luckily, once Claire emerged from behind the screen looking flustered but presentable, Aunt Clarice made a beeline for him and had his neck scarf unknotted and retied correctly in a matter of seconds.

His expression of shock must have showed. "I was costume mistress for the Lagniappe Theater Company for forty years. You look like you could go on stage for a revival of *Showboat.* Clearly, you're a fine actor if you got past those bulldogs. Have you ever considered a second career in the theater?"

He was saved from having to come up with a pithy reply when Claire grabbed her aunt's arm and moved her closer to the CD player, which was still on.

"Why did you come bursting up here?"

Her aunt pressed her hand to her generous bosom. "Oh, right! I saw her, *cher.* Downstairs. Bold as brass, sashaying out to the back verandah with a man half her age."

"Who?" Michael asked.

But Claire didn't need any further explanation. Her worried expression instantly transformed into keen anticipation.

"You're sure?"

Her aunt dug between her breasts and retrieved a handkerchief, which she waved as if in surrender. "*Cher,* I may have trouble remembering faces, but when you give me a person's measurements, I can spot them from one-hundred paces. She's a classic size ten. Thirty-six inch bust, twenty-eight and a half inch waist, forty inch hip. Her shoulders are broad like a swimmer's and she's got long legs for a woman who is only five-eight. I'm telling you. She's your girl."

Claire clapped her hands together. "This might truly be our lucky night, interruptions notwithstanding."

She turned to her aunt, who was panting with exertion now that her adrenaline had eased.

"Do you have the papers?"

The older woman lifted her arm, revealing a dangling draw-string purse.

Claire unwound it from her aunt's wrist, then dug beyond the powder compact and lipstick and removed a cardboard bottom. Beneath it, she took out a thick square of folded papers, backed with tell tale legal-blue.

"Great," she said, then glanced down at her costume and realized she didn't have anywhere to hide the papers. She tried shoving them in the thin pockets of her skirt, but the delicate folds couldn't mask the stiff, sharp shape.

She glanced at Michael and slipped the document into his jacket, then gave his chest a confident pat.

"And those are?"

"The termination of parental rights papers my client needs his ex-wife to sign. He travels a lot for his job and he needs his new wife to formally adopt the children Josslyn Granger abandoned four years ago."

Disgust must have shown on his face, because Claire reached up and smoothed her hand over his cheek, her jade eyes darkening even as her voice dropped to a sensual timber that reheated his simmering blood.

"Cheer up, Murrieta. Once she signs, my case is over. And then, I'm all yours."

CLAIRE TOOK A deep breath and willed herself back into character while Michael swung open the door to the hall. They'd come up with a quick story to explain why he and his new "mistress" had been called away from their rendezvous, but once outside, they found no one around to question their departure.

Maybe their luck had finally turned?

With a slight bow and a twinkle in his eyes, Michael offered his arm. Claire flushed down to her toes. The minute her hands slipped around his impressive pecs, she mourned Aunt Clarice's interruption. Yes, she'd instructed her aunt to be on the watch for her client's former wife. Yes, she'd told her to move heaven and earth to alert Claire if she spotted the woman anywhere among the hundred or so people in attendance. Yes, she needed to put this case to rest so two kids could have the mother they deserved instead of the one they'd gotten stuck with.

But God Almighty, couldn't Clarice have waited just ten more minutes?

Of course, her aunt had had no way of knowing that Claire had been seconds away from guiding Michael into her willing, wanting body. The pounding vibration of her unfulfilled lust still thrummed between her legs, at the center of her belly, in the tips of her breasts.

Even after they'd retreated to the bedroom and she'd realized they were being watched, she hadn't imagined she'd actually want to have sex with him. Heavy petting, sure. Why not? He was hot. And a damned good kisser, whether he was plying his lips against hers or moving them lower. But going all the way with a law enforcement type she'd never met before tonight while they each pretended to be someone they weren't?

That pushed even her limits—and she didn't have that many of them.

Well, she did have a few. She didn't date actors. Her father had been an actor; her mother a playwright. They'd lived, breathed and existed solely for the theater to the point where Claire, an unexpected and unplanned pregnancy, went from doted-on infant to curly-haired prop by the time she was two, pulled out for display at family productions otherwise known as Christmas, Easter and Mardi Gras.

The rest of the time, she lived with Clarice, enjoying a relatively normal childhood that included attending Catholic school, learning to cook and playing sports with the other kids who ran around the French Quarter as if it were the best playground in the universe.

Claire had figured out quickly that nearly everyone orbiting her parents—from bit players to temperamental directors—were masters of the lie. It was second nature for them to fool audiences into believing truths that did not exist. Trouble was, they often transferred their talent into real life. When her parents were around, Claire wasn't sure which parts of her childhood were real and which had been staged for a maximum emotional response.

Luckily for her, she'd gravitated to the stage crews: the carpenters and production hands and costumers like Clarice whose jobs depended on understanding both the magic of make-believe and the very real limitations that reality brought into the world.

Without a doubt, Michael Murrieta would have fit

in well with them. Even now he radiated the character traits she'd associate with an early eighteenth century man of means in New Orleans: confidence, power and sensuality. As they passed people in the halls, he gave the men superior, knowing nods and charmed the ladies with saucy winks or cryptic half smiles. They were half-way across the dance floor, heading toward the verandah that wrapped around the back of the house, when she couldn't take it any longer and stopped his flirting with a smack of her aunt's fan to his shoulder.

"Cut it out," she said.

He swallowed his laughter even as he patted her hand. "Excuse me?"

"You're drawing too much attention," she admonished, not exaggerating. Scores of gazes followed them as they moved across the room, sidestepping dancers and avoiding the small groups of men and women who had clustered together while they sipped brandy or noshed on canapés delivered by white-gloved waiters.

"They're looking at you, not me," he replied.

She snorted, then covered her unladylike response with a flutter of her fan.

"Are you always this smooth?" she asked.

"Actually, I don't think anyone's ever called me smooth."

His chest had puffed up. Claire liked that she'd done that to him—and that it mattered.

"I can't imagine," she replied. "You've blended in here without a seam showing."

They arrived at the tall paned doors that opened out onto the covered porch. When Michael focused his charismatic smile solely on her, her knees wavered.

"That remains to be seen."

Clarice, who'd been following unobtrusively behind them, pointed out the direction Josslyn had gone.

"Thank you," Claire said to her aunt, then kissed her on each cheek. "You still have my phone and my keys?"

"Yes, of course."

"Good. Now, go home. I'll call you once we're done."

"What? I will n—"

Michael slid his hand over her aunt's shoulder. "Trust me, *madame*. Your charge is in safe hands with me. From this point, she's under my protection. Nothing will happen to her."

Clarice narrowed her dark eyes at him, then with a huff, accepted their orders and bustled her way back across the dance floor.

Though September, the weather was sultry. Few couples had ventured outside, where the music from the six-piece orchestra surrendered to the sounds of the Louisiana countryside—the chirp and whine of crickets, the rustle of Spanish moss in the towering oaks, the occasional booming croak of a bullfrog lazing in the center of a glossy pool. In the distance, they heard the distinct sound of a woman's throaty laughter.

They followed, their footsteps muffled by the grassy moss that had grown over the lopsided tiles leading from the house into the maze of tall, trimmed hedges. As they moved farther away from the light, Claire felt Michael's muscles tense.

She glanced behind them. No one was following. No one was even watching. She had no reason to continue holding on to him, and yet pulling away had to be the hardest thing she'd done all night.

After another couple of steps, Michael grabbed her. In the darkness, she nearly gasped, but he pressed a finger to her mouth, stifling the sound. The moon, more than half full, provided just enough light for her to see him nod his head to the left. They stepped off the path and after a few more minutes discovered a break in the hedges.

Within a private garden, the woman they'd followed stood atop a circular terrazzo dais. She untied the knots at the shoulders of her Grecian-styled dress and then slowly, enticingly, allowed the material to fall into a dark pool of silk at her feet.

Unabashed and completely naked, she fanned her long hair over her bare breasts, then posed as if she were a statue of Venus. The men—there were two now, the younger one who had escorted her here and an older man who had clearly been waiting—circled her with hunger in their every step.

The older man wore only pants and boots. The other man remained clothed except for his discarded cravat.

"You're killing us, woman," the nearly naked man complained, his arousal obvious even with his pants on, particularly when he grabbed his crotch and squeezed. "Make your choice. Put one of us out of our misery."

The woman laughed again. This time she threw her wavy extensions over her shoulder so that her dark, silver-dollar sized areola puckered proudly. She slid her hands up her torso, encircling her flesh with her hands and thrusting the upturned nipples even higher.

"Why do I have to choose? Why can't I have you both?"

The men exchanged lascivious glances. The younger man hesitated a moment, then both of them began stripping away their clothes. The older man was thicker around the middle, but his penis more than made up for a bit of paunch.

Claire swallowed hard, her mouth dry.

Now who was the voyeur?

7

MICHAEL MOVED IN closer behind her, his hand protectively splayed on her stomach. She was instantly aware of everything about him, from the citrus scent of his shampoo to the leathery aroma of his boots. Through his clothes, he radiated heat, from his possessive touch to his resilient erection pressed intimately against her backside.

When he leaned forward to whisper in her ear, the insistent thudding of her accelerated heartbeat nearly masked his words.

"We should go."

She shook her head, bracing her hand over his in a move that gave her the contact with his skin that she craved and at the same time stemmed the fluttering in her stomach. She wasn't even sure if this woman was Josslyn Granger. She forced herself to focus on the woman's face and not the pouting roundness of her breasts, the imperfect yet sensual curve of her belly and the pear-shaped hips and thighs.

Her client had sent Claire numerous pictures of his wife, but none like this. She called on all her powers of observation to make the connection between the demure woman in a wedding gown or the sweet young mother with her toddler and the brazen sex goddess being worshipped by her duo of lovers.

But it was Josslyn. Claire could see it in the eyes. In the chin and cheekbones.

Enough for her to know that the woman being pleasured by two men, out in the open where anyone might see, was the woman she needed to find.

The older man stepped behind Josslyn on the dais, exactly the way Michael was poised behind Claire. But instead of holding the woman steady, he surrounded her generous breasts with his huge hands, then proceeded to caress, pluck and play with her nipples. At her feet, the younger man retrieved her gown and then shockingly drew the material up to her waist, knotting the fabric like a belt. While the man behind her buoyed her breasts in offering, the other one suckled her until she arched back and cooed.

They were talking. The older man spoke English, but his companion's words jumbled in some language that Claire couldn't recognize, not with her brain fuddled by what she was seeing—what she was feeling. The thudding in her ears intensified when the younger man dropped to his knees and climbed underneath the woman's skirt.

With a squeal of delight, Josslyn hooked her knee over his shoulder. The sounds of the man feasting echoed against the mossy cobblestones.

Claire's body ignited, her center throbbing as blood rushed to her clitoris. Behind her, she could feel Michael respond as well, his penis lengthening and hardening. She'd nearly had him inside her, and she still desperately craved to make it happen.

When he moved to step back, she stopped him. She

needed to feel his rigid length cradled between the curve of her buttocks.

She needed him.

Claire had seen public displays of carnality before—any dark alley on a weekend in the Quarter provided quite the education. But she'd never been so turned on by it. There was something about the garden, the moonlight and the utter sexual abandon in the woman's face that caught her entirely unaware, snaring her in a rush of need.

"Is it her?" Michael asked, both of his hands now lightly encircling her waist, as if he was afraid to touch her, afraid to mimic the trio playing out an erotic tableau only twenty paces away.

Claire nodded.

"Do you want to leave?"

She hesitated, then shook her head.

No, she didn't want to leave. She most definitely did not want to leave.

"Does this excite you?"

She nodded again.

"Two men. Is that your fantasy?"

She didn't move, unable to answer. She'd always considered herself a free thinker when it came to pleasure, but she'd never been much into porn and had certainly never had sex with more than one guy at a time. She'd truly never imagined either the logistics or the decadent possibilities of four hands and two tongues on a woman's willing body.

Watching men touch, tease and pleasure a woman unhampered by any expectations beyond orgasm pushed Claire to the edge of her comfort zone. Had she ever truly been that free? That wild? That open to the endless possibilities of sensual ecstasy? When Michael spread his hands along her waist, the tips of his fingers caressing the underside of her breasts, she fell into a twirling abyss.

He pulled her flush against him. His every taut muscle enflamed her, swirling her into a maelstrom of conflicting emotions that ranged from shock at what she was witnessing to the reignited passion of having Michael's hands on her. His palms smoothed down the soft folds of her dress, stopping at her thighs, where he inched the material of her skirt upward as if they were gathered curtains being pulled above a stage. He bared her flesh to the elements with such incremental slowness that she registered the sultry air on her skin one body part at a time. First, her ankles. Then her shins. Knees. Thighs.

Claire retreated into the part of herself that did not overthink, did not rationalize, did not judge. She only wanted to feel what he offered, experience what she needed.

"Hold this," he said.

She latched on to the gathered hem and held tight. Through the foliage, she watched the woman on the dais yank up her skirt and swing the material behind her so she could watch the man feasting at her core, his fingers stretching her labia, her sex pink and swollen. Through the pounding in her ears, Claire heard her demand that he lick deeper, harder, faster.

His partner took the bulky skirt over his arm and grabbed at the woman's ass, kneading the flesh hungrily. She cried out as his fingers disappeared between her cheeks, spreading them. He ground his pelvis against her, simulating what he wanted to do to her—what he would likely do to her very, very soon.

The instant the men ripped away the rest of her dress,

Michael's gentle touch inched through the slit in Claire's bloomers.

She was wet. She was hot. Unlike the man ravishing the woman in front of them, Michael was passionately hesitant, his finger skillfully soft. He teased her with his touch, exploring every curve before finally breaching the fold between her outer needs and her inner desires.

He was not rough. He was not desperate. He was tentative. Sweet. And oh-so-precise.

"I'd never share you," he whispered, the pad of his finger connecting with her tiny swollen center. "But it's hot to watch. Look at how she wants it. Look at the way they're focused entirely on her. On her pleasure."

Claire slipped her hand over his. For an instant, he stilled his touch, but she curved her fingers and showed him precisely what to do. He was a quick study, following her lead in toggling her clit with circular motions that blinded her to anything beyond her own growing need. When he slipped his finger inside her, she gasped.

"Yes, Michael. Please."

This was insane. This was lurid. This was amazing. For an instant, she became aware again of the theater of sexual debauchery being played out in front of her. One of the men had dropped onto the dais and, using it like a chair, sat Josslyn down on his lap, facing outward. His hands dug into her hips and he held her at the perfect angle to pump inside her while the man still standing kneaded her breasts as she licked his penis like a popsicle.

But as Claire's arousal edged toward madness, she no longer cared about anyone else's pleasure. She closed her eyes tight and focused on the feel of Michael's hands on her body. Slowly, worshipfully, he touched her, mur-

muring in her ear, making confessions she wasn't sure he'd reveal at any other time or place.

"I couldn't watch another man touch you," he said. "Even if you wanted it. Even if you begged me. God, you're so hot. I want to be inside you, Claire. I want to feel you come. Will you give me that? Come on. Let go."

He slipped a second finger inside her, stretching her, filling her, curling his hand so that he touched her precisely in the right spot. He intensified his reach and tempo, building a friction Claire could not fight. Her orgasm built like a silent wave, washing over and through her until she was shaking so hard in his arms, he had to tighten his grip to hold her still while the sensations climaxed and then receded.

From what seemed like a great distance, she heard grunts, groans and cries as the three people on the dais reached their own peaks. Thankfully, Michael made sweet shushing sounds in her ears that covered their animalistic cries.

"That's it, honey. I can't wait to have more. To have all of you. All to myself."

As the quivers subsided, she allowed herself to relax completely against his strong body. After a few moments, while he righted her skirts and nibbled on her neck, Claire realized that she couldn't wait, either.

CLAIRE MIGHT HAVE been the one to orgasm, but Michael knew that he was the one who'd lost his mind. Something about this place, something about Claire had seeped into his brain and destroyed every rule for behavior he'd ever established for himself.

And it rocked.

He'd never been a prude, but he'd always kept his sexual liaisons private. Maybe because his father had been such a player before he'd met Michael's mother, Michael had never exchanged locker room talk with his buddies or pursued the easy girls in school so he could add another notch to his bedpost. Even in his adult life, he'd only been to strip clubs for bachelor parties or stake-outs. In his mind, sex belonged in the bedroom.

And the sooner he got Claire into one, preferably one without cameras, the better.

Because as crazy as tonight had been, he knew he'd go completely mad if he did not make love to her the right way.

His way.

"He's coming," Claire whispered.

The older man had grabbed his clothes, and after giving Josslyn one last, long, deep-throated kiss, was jogging in their direction. Michael spun Claire around a thick tree trunk and hoped the sound of the man's chuckling didn't mean they'd been made.

The next voice, however, proved that they had.

"You can come out now," Josslyn called, her voice full of amusement.

Claire glanced over her shoulder at him, her eyes wide.

He shrugged. "We've come this far. And clearly, she's not shy."

Though she chewed on her lip for a moment, Claire nodded and slipped around him, leading the way to a break in the foliage that allowed them entrance into the hidden courtyard.

Josslyn remained draped across the younger lover, her back against his chest. He'd buoyed himself into a semi-sitting position on his elbows and the two of them resembled a living, breathing statue that might have been titled, *Lovers Spent*. Michael imagined that if the guy were feeding her grapes instead of lazily playing with her passion bruised nipples, the whole scene would be a lot less lurid.

"You're new here," Josslyn said.

When Claire didn't immediately speak, the woman laughed, giving her lover a chance to nibble on her neck.

"No need to be shy, darlings. You could have joined in if you wanted to. We're all here for one reason, aren't we?"

"Not exactly," Claire said. "Could we talk? Alone?"

Josslyn frowned. "Why? I'm sure that," she turned to her lover and asked in what sounded like Portuguese, "what is your name again, darling?"

The man chuckled. "Leon."

"I'm sure Leon here is trustworthy, aren't you, my great rutting stud?"

The naked man growled, grabbed at her hips and twisted her around until they were practically wrestling in a tangle of limbs and appendages that Michael had seen more than enough of. He grabbed the guy's discarded pants and tossed them onto the dais.

"This won't take long, Ms. Granger. The sooner you give us a few minutes, the sooner you can get back to your fun."

Michael kept his face immobile as Josslyn turned her attention from her lover to him. Her gaze was boldly sexual, even a little hungry, though Michael couldn't imagine she'd want anything more after having two guys filling her two main orifices only a few minutes ago.

When he was hidden behind the bushes with Claire, the woman's sexual abandon had been hot. Now it was a little unnerving. He supposed most things that looked erotic from a distance weren't quite so palatable close up.

She made a grand excuse to her lover, though Michael wasn't entirely sure the guy understood, judging by his squinted response. Josslyn got the message across by patting his cheek and kissing him sloppily while she pressed his clothes to his chest. The man winked at them, then disappeared.

"Don't use that name here," she snapped the minute the guy was out of earshot. "Luckily, Leon speaks only Portuguese and knows me as Dalinda."

"Your real name is only necessary one more time," Claire said, holding out her hand to Michael, who produced the legal document from his pocket. "Sign this and you'll never have to hear that name again."

Josslyn drew her hands through her long hair and thrust out her breasts, eyeing Michael as if to gauge his interest.

He looked away.

"I can't believe I'm being served at a *Nouvelle Placage* event. Do these people have no security?"

Claire pasted on a sweet grin, much more in keeping with the character she'd adopted for the weekend than the woman Michael was quickly—and intimately—getting to know.

"They have great security," Claire said. "We're just good at breaching it. This is a legal document relinquishing your legal rights to the children you abandoned when you left your marriage and divorced their father. His new wife wants to adopt them. For that to happen, you need to sign."

Josslyn made a little show of flipping through the pages, then looked up at Claire and made a sweeping gesture to indicate her nudity. "I don't have a pen."

Claire turned to Michael, but he didn't have anything to sign with, either. The only thing in his pockets was his credentials, and he didn't think flashing an FBI badge to the woman was going to help Claire's case.

"We'll go back up to the house," Claire suggested.

"We will not," Josslyn argued. "Well, you can go if you want, but not with me."

She snatched her dress from the floor and tossed it over her head. Retying the Grecian-styled garment proved impossible, so she simply let it hang from her shoulders, her breasts exposed and her backside barely covered.

"I have a persona here, one I've worked years to establish. The people in this world don't know anything about my past and I don't want them to. I'm not that woman anymore. I haven't been for a long time."

"Then why won't you sign?" Claire challenged.

Josslyn tossed the documents back at Claire. "I haven't seen or spoken to my ex since the divorce. I don't think about him. I didn't even know he was married again. Thank God he's finally moving on."

"But your kids can't."

"His kids," she corrected. "They don't need me. And trust me, they don't want me."

"Then sign the papers. Stay here with my…friend," Claire suggested, "and I'll run up to the house and get a stupid pen."

Josslyn's eyes brightened, her tongue swiping her lips.

"Or I can go," Michael cut in.

The woman sneered, then turned to Claire, who impaled her with a *don't even think about it, sister* look that made it hard for Michael to keep a straight face.

"Don't bother," Josslyn said, her tone lazy, but Michael watched her shift her weight from foot to foot, her gaze focused somewhere over their shoulders. She was playing bored and disinterested, but the act wasn't entirely convincing. Not to a trained observer.

"You won't sign?" Claire asked, incredulous.

"Not here. I told you, I don't want my two lives intersecting again. Tomorrow."

"Where?" Michael asked.

"I have a car. I'll meet you in the city."

"At my office," Claire started to say, but Michael stopped her with a hand to her shoulder.

"I'd rather you not conduct business anywhere so... obvious," he said, hoping she'd understand that while he had no problem helping her put this case to rest, he wasn't forgetting—not for a minute—that a criminal had her in his sights. If the Bandit was staking out Claire's usual haunts, Michael didn't want her anywhere near them until they had a plan to smoke the guy out.

"Right," she said, cottoning on quickly. "Where are you staying?"

"Here," Josslyn answered, then grinned. Only those in the upper echelons of *Nouvelle Placage* remained at the main house the entire weekend. The rest scattered to nearby bed and breakfast inns or hotels. "I know important people."

"In the biblical sense," Michael muttered, which resulted in Josslyn smiling like a Cheshire cat.

"Precisely. And none of those important people know about my life before. I want to keep it that way."

"Fine," Claire said, her tone a bit impatient. "There's a cemetery between here and the city, about twenty miles right off the main highway. It's called St. Honoria. Meet us at the south entrance."

"A cemetery?" Josslyn's lip curled.

"You want to kill off Josslyn Granger for good, so why not? Besides, it's the closest semi-public spot around here and none of the people from *Nouvelle Placage* have any reason to be there. It's secluded, but not abandoned. There are tourists and caretakers."

"What time?" Josslyn stretched languorously. "I intend to be up very late tonight."

Claire rolled her eyes and sighed with impatience.

"Eleven?" Michael suggested.

He really did not like this woman any more than Claire did—and he wasn't entirely sure why. He supposed she was attractive in an *I've-fucked-about-a-hundred-guys-in-my-lifetime* sort of way. Michael appreciated women who owned their sexuality, but those who treated it like a sport weren't his type.

"That's fine," Josslyn said. "Eleven o'clock. And don't forget a pen."

She struggled with her dress a few more minutes, and once she'd finally manipulated her breasts into the material, she patted her wrecked hair and disappeared into the night.

"She's not going to show," Claire said the minute Josslyn was out of earshot.

Michael turned, surprised by the defeat in her voice. "Why do you think that?"

"Why would she? God, I'm so stupid. I can't believe I forgot the pen in Aunt Clarice's purse. I was so concerned with not getting caught, I totally screwed up."

"You're a lot of things, Claire, but stupid isn't one of them. Everyone makes mistakes from time to time. But she'll show. She wants to put that life behind her. If she doesn't sign, her ex will keep trying to track her down."

Claire didn't say anything else. A thick silence engulfed them, one scented with the sex and sweat of people Michael couldn't care less about. He gravitated to Claire, inhaling as he neared so he could cleanse his nostrils with her clean, sensual aromas.

"Let's get out of here." He offered his arm in a way that no longer felt antiquated.

But Claire didn't accept. She stepped away and circled the dais, her brow furrowed, her stare locked on the terrazzo, still slick with fluids he didn't need a crime scene tech to identify.

"Could you do that?" she asked.

"What? Share a woman with another dude? No way."

When she looked up at him, her expression was devoid of humor. "Why not? She's beautiful and sexy and wouldn't want anything by way of commitment. Seems to me she's any man's dream lover."

Michael chewed on his tongue a minute, knowing he had to say this right or he'd come off as a liar—or worse, a hypocrite. "Sharing a woman like Josslyn would be easy for most guys because it's not hard to share something that doesn't mean anything. They fucked hard. They got off on the mechanics—the hands, dicks, vaginas, nipples. Everyone has those body parts. Everyone can have freaky sex."

"But everyone doesn't," she said.

"If I had to choose between freaky sex with some chick I don't give a damn about and slow, sensual, me on top, her tight underneath, missionary, vanilla sex with a woman like you, I'd choose the second. Wouldn't you?"

She stared at him, her eyes wide, her lips parted. "Yeah. Definitely."

"Besides," Michael said, stepping close to the dais to stop her from her mindless rotation. "If some guy tried to touch you while you were with me, I'd break his neck. I might not have four hands and two dicks, but I make the most of what I've got."

She ran her hand gently down his cheek, a smile lighting her eyes to hypnotic green. "You definitely do. Still," she continued, breaking away from him and recircling the terrazzo stage, as if she was caught up in a whirlpool, "it was hot. Watching."

"Not nearly as hot as feeling you come undone."

If not for the bluish tinge of the moonlight, he might have seen her blush. Instead, she chewed on her bottom lip. "Yeah, that was…intimate."

"More intimate than what we were watching."

She sighed. "I don't know what's gotten into me tonight. You have no reason to believe me, but I'm not usually so easy."

"I don't think there's anything about you that's easy, Claire. In fact, you may be the toughest woman I've ever had the pleasure of…being with."

"You're sweet."

"I'm not being sweet, I'm being honest."

"But still—"

Michael had had enough. In any other place, at any other time or with any other woman, he might have responded to her discomfort by apologizing for crossing the line and then asking her to forget what had happened between them. By encouraging her to pull back into her own comfort zone, he could do the same.

But Claire wasn't any other woman—and Michael wasn't the same man he'd been before he met her. He didn't know if it was the family ring, the case, the setting, the lady herself or a combination of everything hitting him at once, but the place where he used to find refuge now only brought him an increased sense of longing.

"Lust is a powerful emotion," he said, forcing himself to have this conversation.

"Clearly," she replied, still circling, still staring, still shaking her head in confusion. "I've lived in New Orleans my whole life. I've seen a lot of salacious shit, but I've never—"

She was near him again—near enough to touch. He snagged her hand, stopping her from going around the dais again. He pulled her close and slid her hand up his chest, neck and chin until he could brush a soft kiss across the inside of her palm.

"Maybe it wasn't what you were seeing that turned you on as much as the company you were keeping."

Her shoulders dropped as a smile again lit those spectacular green eyes.

"Good comeback."

"Thanks. Now, you've done all you can to work your case tonight. Think we can get the hell out of here?"

"And go where?"

"A safe house," Michael assured her. "My unsub isn't going to find you tonight."

"But he will find me."

Michael slipped his arm around her waist and guided her out of the secret garden. "Yes, but not until I say so."

8

THE RIDE BACK to New Orleans took no more than an hour, but as Claire watched the sensual Louisiana countryside with its towering oaks and draping moss turn first into a stark industrial area and then into boxy neighborhoods that ranged from high end to low rent, she found it easy to imagine that days instead of hours had gone by since she'd driven with her aunt in the opposite direction. She definitely wasn't the same woman she'd been when she'd headed to the *Nouvelle Placage* gathering—and not because of the *ménage a trois* she'd witnessed or the orgasm she'd experienced while hidden in the dark foliage nor the fact that she'd found the woman she'd been looking for, but failed to get her signature because of a rookie mistake.

It was all of that.

It was more than that.

It was Michael.

Without turning her head, she watched his profile flash in and out, illuminated by the headlights from passing cars. His strong, dimpled chin added a quirky charm to what otherwise would have been a hard, classically handsome face. He had broad shoulders, strong hands and a chest she could imagine herself lying across naked for hours. His dark blue gaze, which twinkled with humor one minute and burned with intense drive the next, was trained solely on the road, both in front of them and behind.

He was in the zone. Full-on, FBI-honed protection mode.

It was exhilarating.

And terrifying.

In many ways, Michael was her polar opposite. He was an FBI agent, which in and of itself meant that he played by a seriously strict rule book and had standards above and beyond a private investigator like herself. She'd been booted from the local police force because she'd been unable to adopt a black-and-white outlook on law enforcement and criminal behavior. Rampaged by scandal and corruption in the past, the brass in her precinct had skewed in the complete opposite direction. Any investigation that might draw them out of a comfortable delineation between right and wrong was ignored. Any case that might put her fellow officers in a questionable spotlight was passed over for crimes that made good and evil as easily distinguishable as hot and cold.

If only life were that simple—that cut and dried.

And yet, despite his professional position, Michael's behavior betrayed a man who would rebel if the right situation presented itself. Whatever Bureau rules he'd ignored tonight, he'd done so for the sole purpose of tracking her down so he could catch a crazed kidnapper. And at the same time that he appeared to embody every one of the basic rules of decorum—hell, the basic rules of dating—he'd touched her intimately less than an hour after they'd met.

And she'd loved every second of it.

Michael pulled off the main highway and negotiated a maze of back roads until they reached a local hotel with a blinking neon sign exclaiming No Vacancy even though the parking lot had only two cars—one of which was missing a left front tire. The maelstrom of sensations she'd experienced tonight, from fear to curiosity to invigoration to utter orgasmic release, had sapped her energy. But when Michael shoved the gear into park, she felt a renewed zing, as if she'd just spotted the finish line after a wickedly long run.

"You okay?"

Michael had turned off the ignition. With his arm draped on the steering wheel and his eyes dark with concern, she had a brief fantasy of herself climbing across his lap and curling against his chest. As it was, his concern wrapped around her like a fleece blanket on a chilly night. It was an unfamiliar experience for a woman who'd grown up in Louisiana and who had never relied on a man—any man—to give her Southern comfort unless it came in a glass with ice.

But Michael put her safety first. He'd put her case first. Her pleasure first. He'd asked how she was a half dozen times since the garden tête-à-tête with Josslyn Granger, and yet, she didn't find his questions cloying or constricting.

Of course, she'd only answered once, insisting she was fine. The rest of the time, she'd waved away his worry, completely caught up in everything that had happened…everything she'd learned. About Josslyn. About the man who was after her.

About herself.

"I'm just exhausted," she confessed.

"Probably low blood sugar," he concluded, giving the

abandoned parking lot a once over before he reached into the backseat and retrieved the sandwiches, beer and bottled water they'd picked up at a local deli a half mile from the hotel. "This will fix it."

Michael insisted she remain in the car while he gathered their food and the bag she'd retrieved at *Nouvelle Placage* from his trunk. Once sure there was no one around, he led her up the open stairway that zigzagged up the side of the hotel.

The room he'd rented was at the end, next to a room marked off with crime scene tape.

She stared at the crisscrossed doorway apprehensively while he used his key.

"Nice digs," she said.

He grinned at her unapologetically. "Only the best."

Inside, the room proved, at the very least, clean. The unmistakable scent of pine disinfectant permeated the place, but once he switched on the air conditioning unit under the window, it dissipated, leaving behind the vague mustiness that only a New Orleans hotel room could possess. Michael waited for her to walk completely inside, then bolted the door behind them, dropped the food off on the pockmarked table between the two double beds and then deposited her bag next to the door to the bathroom.

"Want to eat first or shower?" he asked.

She eyed the two beds and with a snicker pictured the scene from *It Happened One Night*. There wasn't much point in erecting a Wall of Jericho between her and Michael tonight, even if they were still relative strangers.

He might not have seen her completely naked, but he'd had open access to every part of her body. Twice.

And he'd made the most of it both times, without the

benefit of a horizontally flat surface. When she started to imagine how he might utilize a mattress to his advantage, she decided to take him up on the shower first—preferably, a cold one.

She beelined straight for the bathroom.

By the time she was back in her favorite Mardi Gras commemorative T-shirt and the panties, she felt like herself again. The only thing missing was her Smith & Wesson 9mm and her jeans. The first she'd left behind so she wouldn't arouse suspicion at the plantation if anyone rooted through her things. The jeans had been abandoned for the sake of comfort. Wasn't like the man hadn't already seen some of her most intimate parts. She wasn't going to be shy now about her bare legs.

When she came out of the bathroom, he was sitting on the bed nearest the window, tapping away on a laptop, a cell phone tucked under his ear.

"Yeah, well, next time I won't check in at all," he quipped to the person on the other end of the phone. "Then you'll be even more gorgeous."

He waited for the response, snorted, then hung up the phone.

She raised an eyebrow. If he had a girlfriend—or worse, a wife—she might just have to kill him, even without her gun.

At first, he only spared her a quick glance, followed by a double-take. His stare locked on her bare legs then rose, millimeter by millimeter, up to her pale pink panties and snug T-shirt, underneath which she wore nothing but skin. Her nipples tightened under his intense scrutiny, and without wanting to, she turned around and pretended to mess with the towel she'd wrapped around her wet hair.

Behind her, he groaned. She chanced a quick look

over her shoulder and saw that while his jaw hadn't exactly dropped open at her exposed ass, there was a slackness in his chin that he neatly covered by clearing his throat.

"That was my partner," he explained. "She said I interrupted her beauty sleep."

"I take it you mean *partner* in the FBI sense," she said, padding across the room.

"If you think I mean it in any other sense after what happened between us tonight, then I'm seriously losing my touch."

"Oh, no," she said, settling on the bed closest to the bathroom. "Your touch is just fine. Better than fine, actually."

She masked the charged silence by towel drying her hair until she was sure she wouldn't drip all over the pillow and comforter. With her fingers, she combed through the conditioner softened strands and hoped she didn't look too much like a drowned rat. She'd washed away the elaborate curls she'd worn for the ball and if she had any luck, her naturally thick hair wouldn't look too ridiculous when it dried.

Judging by the way he continued to steal glances at her, she must have looked tasty enough to eat.

Which reminded her...

She grabbed the brown bag he'd dropped on the night stand and unwrapped the muffaletta sandwich they'd bought at an all-night deli, portioned a quarter of the massive round Italian bread stuffed with meat and olive spread onto a pile of napkins.

When he didn't accept his piece, she realized his gaze was still stuck on her lower torso. She touched his arm. The electric current between his flesh and hers made her catch her breath.

For a split second, she considered chucking the food aside and making a meal out of him instead. He curved his hand around hers, took the sandwich and set it aside, then concentrated on slowly easing the tension out of her fingers.

The charged sensation running up and down her arm was no longer shocking—but it was just as powerful.

She cleared her throat and pulled away. This wasn't the time. It was certainly the place, what with two beds at their disposal, but they had a lot to talk about. What he'd told her while under surveillance at the plantation house had been enough to establish trust, but now, she needed details.

Lots and lots of details—particularly the type that would keep her from launching herself across the mini-divide between the beds and jumping his bones.

She popped the tops on the beer and slid his bottle across the table, avoiding further contact. She ached to find out just how hot they'd be together now that they weren't undercover, on display or under the influence of sex so blatant and raunchy, they'd reacted without thinking. If they made love before the sun came up, it would be simply because they wanted to.

And she really, really wanted to.

"Now that we're entirely alone," she said, forcing her brain away from all matters sexual, "tell me everything you know about The Bandit. When and how did he first come to the attention of the FBI?"

He picked up his sandwich and chewed a mouthful, took a swig of his beer, then wiped his hands on one of the extra napkins. The muscles in his neck and shoulders relaxed, as if he too was thankful for a topic that might break the seductive spell attempting to lace them together like two sides of her abandoned corset.

"Over a year and a half ago," he explained, "the unsub my colleagues dubbed The Bandit made the mistake of striking in the same community twice, in a relatively small town just outside of San Diego."

He leaned back against his pile of flattened pillows, looking so comfortable in his skin, she couldn't help but want to climb in beside him. Instead, she grabbed a bottle of water and sucked down half the contents. How weird would it be if she dumped the rest over the top of her head?

"The police force there was small," he continued. "Four officers, two patrol cars, no resources. The first incident, to be honest, they kind of blew off. A woman claimed to have been kidnapped and kept against her will for three days. There was no evidence of rape, and because she had a history of alcohol problems, they figured she'd just gone on a bender. But the second woman got their attention. Church secretary, married, two kids. No connection to the first woman except that they lived in the same zip code. But as the town has only one zip code, that wasn't saying much."

"Typical," Claire commented. "Another community where only upstanding citizens qualify as crime victims."

"At least it didn't take a third victim to get their attention," he said. "Small town cops rarely want feds on their turf. But they'd recovered scarves like the one you received, black with the blood red Z's, and they recognized a signature and called for the FBI. But it wasn't a federal case yet, so we were only notified of the possibility that a serial rapist was working in California."

"And you got the initial call?"

He took another generous bite of the sandwich and chewed while he shook his head. "I'm based in San Francisco. I didn't get called until the San Diego Bureau established that the unsub had attacked across state lines. By then, there were four victims. Two in California, one in Arizona and one just outside Vegas. The more information they gathered from the women, the more it looked like the guy had some sort of Antonio Banderas fixation. That's when I was brought in."

"Why you? Are you some sort of Zorro expert?"

He glanced at the ceiling, chuckling. "Something like that."

She put her sandwich down and regarded him carefully. His answer was purposefully vague. Just what was he hiding?

"You were better at bending the truth a couple of hours ago," she said.

When his eyes met hers, she felt an added punch of intensity behind his dreamy baby blues. "Let's just say that my superiors noticed my movie posters and memorabilia. My father was an avid collector. I've read all the Johnston McCulley books, seen all the movies and television shows. They decided I was the perfect agent to get inside this guy's head."

"And are you?"

He swiped the crumbs off his folder and into a nearby trashcan, then pulled a book out from under one of his piles of paperwork.

The leather was so battered and old that she couldn't read the faded title on the spine, but expected it to be a first edition of *The Curse of Capistrano,* which for some reason, she knew was the first novel to detail the exploits of the man in black.

But when she tilted the book beneath the dim lamp

on the side table and turned to the first page, she read, *The Amorous Adventures of Joaquin Murrieta.*

Murrieta?

"A relative?" she asked, scanning down the page until she found the publication date inscribed at the bottom: 1875.

"Joaquin Murrieta was the son of a Spaniard raised in Chile who came to California as a young man seeking his fortune any way he could get it."

"And someone wrote a book about his love life? Why?"

Michael retrieved the book, flipped a couple of pages, then handed it back to her so she could read a yellowed piece of newsprint tucked inside—a single column published over fifty years after the book.

The type, off-kilter in the way that old documents often were, swam under her weary eyes, but she skimmed enough to realize that Joaquin Murrieta was the man upon whom the iconoclastic, uber-romantic, black-clad, sword-and-whip wielding masked bandit of colonial California was based.

"You're kidding, right?" she asked, unable to reconcile the light-eyed, chiseled All-American man sitting across from her with the tall, dark and dangerous *hombre* of legend. "You can't be his great-great-grandson."

"No," Michael said, chugging a healthy mouthful of beer. "That would make me over a hundred years old. I'm actually his great-times-five grandson. One of three. I have two older brothers."

She shook her head in disbelief. She'd never for an instant considered that the character who'd become an icon of American justice was based on a real person— particularly not one related to the man who looked like the poster boy for apple pie.

"So, let me get this straight. This serial criminal has delusions with black capes and Z's carved into walls, so the FBI picks up one of the real Zorro's relatives to go after him?"

"That about sums it up."

She paged through the book and found an inked drawing of Joaquin Murrieta, whose wild eyes, flyaway mane and jaunty hat made him look every bit the Hispanic rogue.

And nothing like Michael.

"There's no family resemblance," she concluded.

Michael turned the book around so he could look at the picture, which she imagined he'd studied about a million times. "I don't know. I bet if he smiled, we'd look just alike. I think the indentation there is a dimple in his chin."

She snatched the book back and looked again. "That's a faded spot on the paper."

He shrugged. "Family resemblance notwithstanding, Joaquin Murrieta is the man upon whom the legend was based. And I'm related to him. This is his ring."

Claire had caught a glimpse of the ring earlier, but assumed it was a part of his costume as much as his breeches and cravat. Intrigued, she took his hand into hers so she could examine the gold band under the dim light.

Bright green and lightly faceted, the stone in the center of the worn gold band looked old and damaged. But after a moment, she realized that what she'd mistaken for an unsightly scratch was actually a crude etching of the letter Z.

"This belonged to him?" she asked, trying to keep her attention on the sparkling turquoise fire that rippled off of the flanking black opals rather than the long, rugged shape of his fingers.

"My father was an art expert, among other things," he replied, his voice a warm whisper. "He traced the ring's ownership back to Joaquin, who won it in a game of chance from a wealthy Spanish nobleman named Don Diego, which is probably where that part of the story came from. Anyway, Pop verified the theories of many historians who believed that the wild-eyed Chilean highwayman was the template for the famous bandit. And now this family story has been perverted by a madman who'd like nothing more than to hold you against your will and rape you, all under the guise of some grand seduction he learned from this book."

The word *rape* scraped inside her ears. It didn't belong in this room. In the intimate space slowly closing in around them as they sat on the bed, his hand in hers, a book of seduction spread open on her bare thighs.

"No one mentioned rape," she muttered.

As a cop, she'd investigated mostly petty thefts, gang shootings or acts of domestic violence. She'd only worked one calculated murder—and that was the one that had ended her career. Even as a P.I., she'd never come across a case as far-reaching and grandiose. Or sick and twisted.

She was out of her league.

Luckily, Michael was not.

"This guy started off as relatively benign, if you consider drugging and kidnapping benign. But he's escalated. He's used my family's history to fuel his sick fantasies and I intend to stop him."

As much as she didn't want to, Claire released Michael's hand in order to pick up the book again. "So this is what, his playbook?"

"Apparently. Murrieta was captured and killed by a cavalry officer back in 1853. But, in 1875, an historian published his account, that discounted the legend that the officer had ordered Murrieta's head to be cut off and kept in a jar."

"That's disgusting," she said.

"Probably an effective crime deterrent, though," Michael admitted. "But the head must have belonged to someone else. According to this and several other sources, after his wife's death in 1853, Joaquin Murrieta retired his mask and lived a long life concentrating on his skills as a lover, not a fighter."

He scooted a couple of inches away from her, for which she was thankful. His leathery, musky scent, peppered with the enticing smells of his sandwich, was making her stomach growl.

"The author tracked down all the women Joaquin supposedly seduced and interviewed them for his unauthorized biography," he continued. "And the unsub somehow got his hands on a copy and is using it as a manual to terrorize women. Women like you."

"But why me?"

Michael fanned through the pages, stopping at the collection of ink drawings and grainy photographs in the center. Various women, some who shared Murrieta's ethnic heritage and many who did not, graced the well thumbed pages. He paused at a photograph of a regal looking, Asian woman with come-hither eyes, then flipped through until he found the portrait of an elaborately dressed woman with milky skin a shade or two darker than Claire's and arrestingly light eyes.

"Here," he said.

Claire read the caption.

Paulette Girard, an actress of some repute in New

York City, traveled to California with her speculator
husband, who died in transit. He left her destitute with
three small children and lonely for male companion-
ship, which Joaquin Murrieta was more than eager to
provide.

As the words tumbled through her brain, she felt her
stomach tense. The story of Paulette's life, which began
here in New Orleans with her birth to a wealthy French
father and a Creole mother, immediately felt familiar.
Personal. Claire curled onto the pillows, barely aware
of Michael announcing he was going to take a shower
as she read about Paulette's renowned beauty and hard-
headed nature that forced her to quit her hometown after
she objected to her father's choice for her husband.

In a great act of rebellion that predated the War Between the States, the barely eighteen-year-old woman
had joined a traveling theater troupe headed North. She'd
left when the antebellum South was still in the midst of
its heyday and never looked back.

Claire paged back to the photograph of Paulette. Did
she look like the woman? Claire didn't think so. Maybe
a little around the eyes, but she hoped she'd never looked
quite that—available. Paulette's almond-shaped gaze seduced the camera, just as any actress's would. But that
didn't mean she was Claire's great-times-five grand-
mother.

Did it?

Claire vaguely remembered her father claiming that
the Lécuyer family had produced a long line of per-
formers, entertainers and actors, going back centuries.
And unless her brain was completely on the fritz from
hunger and exhaustion, she seemed to recall that her
great-grandfather's first name had been Girard.

Paulette Girard. Her ancestor. A lover of Joaquin Murrieta.

Now she understood why the Bandit had targeted her—and the truth chilled her to the bone.

9

MICHAEL STALKED INTO the bathroom and stripped off his clothes. As he expected, Claire had been instantly engrossed by the book. It was sordid and salacious, but at the same time, grandly romantic. Even a guy like him, who had never had many serious relationships, had been blindsided by the stories about his randy ancestor and the exotic ladies he'd lured in to his bed.

Paulette Girard might have been one of many lovers Joaquin had toyed with, but she had stood out from the pack. She hadn't fallen into the Latin lover's arms easily. He'd had to work for her.

Hard.

For the first time since Michael had discovered the book in his father's collection, he understood what his ancestor had experienced when he'd fallen under the spell of the shrewd, yet painfully beautiful Paulette. He'd wanted her with a need not unlike a drowning man for oxygen. He was willing to do anything to possess her, even for one night.

For Claire, Michael had already put his career at risk. He'd broken protocol by paying his way into the sex fetish club without authorization. He was positive his superiors would have preferred if he'd simply gone in and flashed his credentials to get Claire. Instead he'd ended up seducing her for the voyeuristic pleasure of people who could use a recording of their bedroom encounter to ruin them both.

To keep Claire out of the Bandit's clutches, he'd taken the risk. He hadn't known her when he'd made the choice, but he'd known enough about her from her file and from the fantasies he'd entertained after reading about her ancestor that she was worth the gamble.

Now that he'd touched her, talked to her, tasted her, he knew one thing for certain—for all he'd put on the line for her, once the danger had passed, she wouldn't think twice about him.

Not that he wasn't a great guy. He knew there were plenty of women who would cherish a man who was hardworking, relatively good-looking and loyal, sometimes to a fault. But Claire fed on danger, uncertainty and adventure—and the only thing he wanted to do was keep her safe. If not for the pesky problem of his criminal record, his brother Danny might be a better match for her.

But Danny wasn't here, was he? Trapped in a cozy hotel room with a woman who'd already come undone at his hand. A woman who'd just knocked on the bathroom door.

"Michael?"

He froze, his hands mid-lather on his chest, when she opened the door.

"Claire?"

"Yeah, sorry," she said, though he didn't hear an ounce of apology in her voice. "I read it all, but I need to know more."

He forced himself to continue with his shower despite

her intrusive presence, which filled the room with more heat and more steam than the piddling showerhead could manage if he'd left it running at full blast all day.

"Okay," he said, clearing the awkwardness from his voice.

He heard the creak of plastic and imagined that she'd closed the toilet seat so she could sit. She was inches away from him, dressed in nothing more than a pale pink scrap of nothing and a T-shirt.

"So you think I'm related to Paulette Girard," she said.

He smoothed the soap into his hair and gave it a rough scrub, trying to ignore the tight pull of his growing erection.

"I have a team of genealogists working the case from Utah, Claire. You are related to her. That's how we found you. All the previous victims were related to women written about in the book. We looked for living descendents and your name came up as one of the likeliest to get a scarf next."

"One of?"

"There are a few others, but they didn't quite fit the victimology. Too old. Too young. He doesn't discriminate in many ways, but you are single, attractive, closest to the age Paulette was when she had her affair with Joaquin."

"And exactly what does he want to do to me?"

Michael rinsed the soapy foam from his face. He didn't want to think about what the unsub wanted with Claire. Not when his brain was swimming with images of what he wanted instead—to throw back the thin shower curtains and tug her into the stall with him.

He resisted, bracing his hands on the cold tile so the water sluiced down the back of his neck. "He wants to possess you. To him, it's a grand seduction, just like Joaquin and Paulette."

Beside him, the curtain rustled. He turned his head, and beyond the thin waterproof fabric, he saw her silhouette. He watched, enthralled, as she grabbed the hem of her T-shirt and lifted it slowly over her head. She then stepped out of her panties.

The only part of his body that managed to move was his erection, which hardened with the kind of pleasurable pain that only sex inspired. She was coming into this cramped shower stall with him, whether he liked it or not.

And the trouble was, he liked the idea very much.

READING ABOUT PAULETTE and Joaquin's affair had, at first, fascinated her. With an interest she'd thought was detached, she'd read how the man had sent the woman rare flowers, exotic sweets and the kind of silk underthings that no respectable lady at the time would ever possess. Paulette had resisted for weeks, leading him on with songs she sang in the cantina where she worked, teasing him by undressing in front of her open window when she knew he was watching, but wouldn't dare come near. He'd actually climbed into her bed uninvited one night and while she'd allowed him to touch her in her most private places, she'd denied him the one thing he wanted most.

Just like Claire had done—completely without meaning to—to Michael.

But she didn't want to deny him any longer. She didn't want to deny herself. Images of the Bandit perverting Joaquin's amorous adventures were like layers of dirt and grime clinging to her skin. She needed another shower to wash it all away.

She needed a shower with Michael.

"Claire," he said, his voice ripe with warning as she climbed past the curtain.

He was magnificent. With his arms braced so that the showerhead sprayed water down his muscled back, she had a perfect view of his long legs, lean thighs and perfect glutes. She ignored the reluctant glance he threw over his shoulder. He wasn't stopping her, was he? He remained stock still, even when she stepped into the water and wrapped her arms around his waist so she could press her cheek against his slick back.

"I can't help it, Michael," she said. "All that reading about seduction got me hot."

She wasn't lying, but it was a gross exaggeration to say that the book alone was responsible for her enhanced libido. The truth was, the book only reminded her how much she'd wanted Michael inside her when they were in the room at the plantation house and how incomplete she'd felt in the garden when he'd brought her to orgasm, but had taken nothing for himself. She speared her hands down his torso and thighs, then back up and around his impressive erection.

"This is what I was missing," she confessed, licking the water off his back while she circled his cock with her palm and tested the length and thickness against her hand. Unbidden, her body quivered with anticipation.

"Claire," he protested, but with a tighter squeeze, she silenced him.

"Give me one good reason why we shouldn't do this, Michael? One good reason not to finish what you started?"

He answered with a groan, a long, drawn-out, throaty sound that corresponded with the rhythm of her hands on his erection. Every inch of his body emanated power—but, equally, he exuded control. Control over everything except what she was doing to him, which was raw and hungry and oh-so-wonderful.

She pressed her body fully against his, appreciating the contrasts of his skin to hers, of his hardness to her softness, of his distinctively male musculature to her decidedly feminine curves. Her nipples scraped against his bare back, igniting needs and wants that had been only fantasies when she'd stood on the other side of the shower curtain. Now, they could all be real, if only he'd surrender to the pull.

With the tips of her fingers, she pressed into the tight V just below his head.

He spun around, breaking her grip, just when he was on the edge of a well-deserved release to match the one he'd given her in the garden. But he didn't seem to want that as much as he wanted to kiss her, because he pressed her tight against the opposite wall and did just that—long and hard, exploring every inch of her mouth with his hot, insistent tongue.

And then his hands were everywhere. The slick heat of the water spread all over her body while he kissed and pleasured her neck, her breasts, her belly and below. The moment his hand made contact with her lust-swollen clit, she cried out in ecstasy. He touched and teased, taunted and tempted until she was wild with need.

She didn't need him to drop to his knees and ply his talented tongue to her belly button, but she certainly didn't stop him when he did. Instead, she ran her hands through his hair, curling her fingers around his ears as the water splashed their bodies, the steam hot in her lungs and yet soothing on her skin. He smoothed his hand down her leg and around her ankle, and before she was aware of what sensual delight he had in store for her, he stood. With her leg hooked over his elbow, he had perfect access. She gasped as the head squeezed into her tight, welcoming body. In one slick stroke, he was inside her, filling her, fulfilling her.

"Yes, yes," she murmured as he found his rhythm, one that danced between slow and torturous. With each slide, he reached deeper into her. With each withdrawal, he awoke another layer of nerve endings she'd forgotten she possessed.

He cupped her breast, teasing her nipple with his thumb as he kissed her until she couldn't differentiate between the moisture of the shower and the liquid heat blasting through her body. She grabbed blindly for any part of him she could reach. His arms. His neck. His chest. His ass. Once she grasped his backside, he thrust deeper and longer, then faster until her mind erupted with an explosion of color and light.

When he released her leg, she was too wobbly to stand. With a chuckle, he buoyed her against his body and swung them both under the stream of water. She curled against him, hungry for the warmth of his caressing kisses.

"Feel clean now?" he asked.

"I feel like a prune, I think," she replied.

He turned off the water and retrieved a towel from the tiny metal shelf in the corner. He wrapped her torso, placing a kiss between her breasts after he tucked in the corner.

"This is cozy," he said, pulling her close.

"This is crazy."

"I'm not the one who came barging into your shower."

"But you thought about it," she guessed.

"I did not," he said, but when he wasn't undercover, Michael Murrieta was a terrible liar.

"Uh-huh," she said, unwinding from his embrace and stepping onto the tiny square of a bath mat, which was pretty much soaked through.

Claire retrieved her T-shirt and panties, then dashed out of the bathroom, determined to give him space while he dried off and dressed. She had no regrets. From the minute he'd spirited her upstairs to the bedroom in the plantation house and she hadn't resisted, they'd been on a path to having sex. Hot sex. Hot, wet sex, that she decided was now her favorite kind.

But most importantly, when she picked up the book she'd abandoned on the bed, she was no longer creeped out by The Bandit or his sick intentions. He wasn't going to get anywhere near her. Not if she had anything to say about it—and definitely not if Michael did.

He came out of the shower a few minutes later wearing a grey T-shirt and loose running shorts. His hair was spiky and his skin flushed so that his blue eyes lasered straight through her.

She smiled as she curled under the covers of her bed. He didn't move. Did he need an invitation? She pulled back the blanket and patted the mattress.

But instead of joining her, he cursed and plopped down on the corner of the bed.

His bed.

The one farthest away from her.

"This shouldn't have happened," he said, running his hand over his face.

"Why not?"

"Because I'm supposed to be protecting you," he argued, his self-recrimination growing with every syllable.

"Well, you did forget about the protection," she chided, though she wasn't worried. She'd been on birth

control for years and doubted that a guy like Michael
went around having indiscriminate sex.

As her words registered, he cursed even louder. "I'm
sorry. I never forget about protection."

Somehow, the fact that he'd been so caught up with
her that he'd forgotten to dig into his overnight bag or
wallet or wherever he stashed his prophylactics pleased
her more than it should have. "Neither do I, ordinarily,
so I guess we're both okay. And I'm on the Pill, so no
worries in that department, either."

He continued to shake his head and Claire imagined
that whatever four-letter words he'd used out loud were
nothing compared to what was going on in his mind.
As she'd surmised earlier, Michael was an honorable
man—a by-the-book, no exceptions guy, even when it
came to sex. She'd pushed him out of his comfort zone,
but refused to feel guilty about it. Wasn't like he didn't
enjoy himself.

"So," she said, settling deeper into the mattress, which
was surprisingly cozy. Sated and deliciously exhausted,
she figured that maybe discussing the next step in his
case would draw him out of his unnecessary self-recrim-
inations. "Tell me how you intend to catch this Bandit."

He narrowed his gaze, and for a second, she felt as if
he was seeing her for the first time. "I think we need to
get some sleep."

In a flash, he'd stacked up his paperwork and shoved
it into a bag he kept beneath the bed. He double checked
the lock on the door, retrieved his firearm and placed it
on the bed stand between them.

"Geez, if you don't want me to climb into bed with
you in the middle of the night, you just have to ask," she
joked, eying the weapon.

Michael frowned. "What? Oh, that's not—"

She laughed out loud. "Jesus, Michael, what's wrong with you? We had sex. Great sex, if I do say so myself. Do you regret it?"

He dropped to his knees at her bedside. His eyes really were an amazing color—like sapphire sparkles atop a Caribbean sea. "God, no, Claire. Are you kidding? If it was up to me, I'd climb into bed with you right now and make love to you for the rest of the night. With protection."

His half-grin eased the sudden and unexpected tightness in her chest.

"Isn't it up to you?" she asked, sliding her hand onto 's cheek. "And me?"

'or an instant, he leaned into her palm, his eyes c his expression so relaxed in her touch, she tho she might have to grab at her chest to keep her hear om cracking a little.

But hen he pulled away, shaking his head as if to dispel the effects of her touch. "In this moment, yes. But the sun's going to rise tomorrow and our actions tonight have already put us at a disadvantage."

"How do you figure?" she asked.

"We had a plan, Claire. A smart, clear-cut plan. First, we meet up with Josslyn in the morning, get her signature and put your case to rest. Then we regroup with Ruby and the local FBI office and work up a plan that lures the Bandit out in the open without putting you at risk."

"And how has our making love changed any of that?"

He turned his face to the ceiling, his jaw tight and his mouth an angry slash across his face. "Because now, I can't put you in danger. I can't let you go meet with Josslyn and, God help me, I can't use you as bait."

Claire jumped out of bed, nearly tripping in her

disorientation. Michael wasn't a stupid man. He wasn't, as far as she knew, a chest beating Neanderthal. So why the hell was he suddenly acting like one?

"Why? Because we had sex? Don't be so provincial, Michael. Just because you fucked me doesn't mean you own me."

He grabbed her by the upper arms, his grip tight and his gaze filled with a hot desperation that went straight into her bloodstream. "I don't have to own you to want to protect you."

He yanked her up so that their lips clashed, and despite her fury, she couldn't resist channeling her anger into the kiss. She fed on his fear for her, filling herself with the knowledge that for her, he'd risk everything— her case, his career…even the safety of other women the Bandit might target next. Though she suspected that before meeting her, Michael Murrieta rarely acted on impulse, that's what he was doing now.

And she had to stop him.

She braced her hands on his face and slowly eased the tension out of her lips and tongue so that the explosion of frantic passion ebbed. With each tender touch and brush of a kiss that followed, her chest ached even more. She'd waited her entire life for someone to care enough about her to put her ahead of everything else, and now she couldn't accept his generosity, even when so honestly offered.

"Michael, I owe it to those kids to make sure Josslyn is out of their lives forever. It's just one little signature that I need. And sooner or later, we're going to have to confront this Bandit freak, because if we don't, other women will be at risk. And even if he moves on to someone new, if he's fixated on me the way that your ancestor was focused on Paulette, he'll just come back for me later."

Michael shut his eyes tight, and on his face Claire saw his struggle between needing to keep her out of harm's way and doing his job—a struggle she guessed he'd have to deal with for as long as he was anywhere near her.

Michael was smart. Once he pushed beyond the euphoria of a great orgasm, he'd realize the truth. The whole truth. Yes, he cared about her, but they were strangers who'd achieved instant intimacy because of circumstances and chemistry. He couldn't throw his career aside for her. And more importantly, he couldn't put other women in danger by ignoring this one shot at catching the Bandit before the man could do more harm.

"He won't give up," she said, driving the final nail into her argument.

He drew her fully against him, wrapping her in a hug that squeezed out any chance that they'd be together once this case was complete. "Then neither will I."

10

THOUGH THEY SLEPT in the same bed that night, Claire was glad their argument over the Bandit, and her insistence that she meet Josslyn this morning as planned, kept them from doing anything more than cuddling. She'd had one-night stands before, but none that had impacted her so deeply in such a short time.

She'd known Michael for less than a day, but she couldn't help but care about him, about his case, about his career, even about his quest to protect his family name. And clearly, he cared about her just as much. Yet despite his reluctance to let her out in public when the Bandit might be watching her, he agreed to accompany her to the cemetery to secure Josslyn Granger's signature on the legal papers so she could close up this case.

But his agreement came at a price. She'd had to listen, late into the night, to every gory detail about what the Bandit had done to the women he'd caught—how he'd drugged them with Rohypnol, spirited them away to an undisclosed location and then messed with their minds until in the end, they believed they'd consented to his sick, sexual game. He'd pulled no punches in explaining how the unsub had confounded all ordinary profiling techniques by borrowing aspects of his modus operandi from three distinct serial killer types, and that it was only a matter of time before he escalated one more level and either mutilated his victim or killed. Or both.

She'd fallen asleep only to be haunted by disturbing, disjointed nightmares filled with black masks and blood red roses whose thorns sliced open her skin in intimate places. And every time she'd gasped awake, he'd held her tight against him until she fell back asleep.

She'd ended up sleeping later than she'd intended, and Michael had let her, wanting her to be fresh and sharp for the meeting. She'd dressed quickly and silently. What he'd told her about the Bandit terrified her, but also made her more determined. Of all the women he might attack, she was the most qualified to deal with him—to beat him. And even beyond her own personal skills, she had Michael. Together, they'd be unstoppable.

At least, until they had no reason to be together at all.

"You'll stay in the car until Josslyn shows up," Michael said as he packed their belongings into the back of his rental.

"And what if Josslyn decides she's not going to show up unless she sees me? This is my case, Michael. I'm not going to hide in the car."

"Did you hear anything I said to you last night?" he asked, his voice clipped.

"I heard every frickin' word. But you're going to be with me the whole time. Even if the Bandit somehow found out about our meeting with Josslyn—and I can't imagine how he could—he won't be able to get near me. A signature only takes a few minutes and this may be my last shot to get it. I'm not taking any chances at scaring her off."

He shook his head, muttering as he crossed to the

passenger side door and held it open for her. "You know, if it's the payment from your client that you're worried about, I could requisition that amount from the FBI."

She was halfway into the car before what he'd said fully registered.

"You did not just say that."

He winced, then slammed the door and went around to the other side. He hesitated before he slid in beside her, then with a curse, got in and shoved the key into the ignition.

She slammed her hand onto the gear shift. There was no way they were going anywhere until he understood her motivations.

Sure, she needed the money from the case. Her business, like so many others in the city, was struggling to survive. But that didn't mean she wasn't personally invested in the cause. If Josslyn Granger disappeared again without signing over her parental rights, her children lost their chance at having a mother who could make medical decisions for them, sign them up for little league or, God forbid, take care of them if anything happened to their father. Josslyn Granger's ex-husband had every right to want his new wife to have parental rights for his children—rights Josslyn had thrown away a long time ago.

Rights Claire's parents had had, but rarely ever used.

A psychologist would have a field day analyzing the motives behind Claire's determination, but that thought had to wait. At the moment she had to convince Michael not to derail her.

"You've called your partner for backup, right? Even if something goes wrong and the Bandit somehow finds out where we're going to be, there's no way he'd make a move. You said it yourself. He might be crazy, but he's not stupid. We'll be out in broad daylight and I'll be surrounded by FBI."

He gingerly picked up her hand, moved it out of his way, then shoved the car into reverse. "I don't understand why you're willing to put yourself in danger for a woman who can't be bothered to see her own kids in years."

"It's for those kids that I'm willing to put myself in danger. They deserve to be rid of this woman. She could flit back into their lives in a year or two and claim visitation, or worse, custody."

"A judge would never—"

"Do you know that? And should her family have to go through the fight? Josslyn abandoned them. She doesn't give a shit about them. All she cares about is her next thrill, her next easy fuck. Let's just get this over with. Then we'll both have what we want."

Relucantly, he turned the vehicle in the direction of the cemetery. Though Michael had locked the pertinent evidence about the case in the trunk of the car, she'd kept the book about Joaquin Murrieta with her. She'd read the entire section about Paulette, but was curious about the other women he'd seduced—the women whose descendents had been captured, terrorized and violated by the Bandit.

"How do you think this guy found the book to begin with?" she asked, hoping that discussing Michael's case might derail his sour mood. "I mean, this isn't exactly on the top of the bestseller lists."

Michael's mouth tightened, but after a few beats, he relaxed. "We don't know for sure, but one possibility is from a man named John Wright Parsons, an avid reader who lived alone in the San Diego area. There are only a few copies in existence and one was at his local library.

No one checked it out for two decades until Parsons used his library card nearly five years ago. He never returned the book."

Claire dug into her purse, looking for her sunglasses. The sky was a brilliant blue and the sun, which had already started steaming the moist air, was going to play havoc with her vision if she didn't find her shades.

"But Parsons isn't your guy?"

Michael produced his own dark glasses from the console between the seats. "He died three years ago at the age of ninety-two, so no. With no family, his house went into probate. According to neighbors, the place turned into a flop house. By the time we got inside, anything that hadn't been bolted down was gone, including the book. Someone could have sold it for cash to a secondhand store or the unsub could have been the actual thief. We don't know."

For the rest of the ride, Claire kept Michael talking about the case. She was struck by how forthcoming he was, even if she suspected he was still trying to scare her into going into hiding. Since this was a moot point, she ignored his possible motivation and concentrated only on the fact that he held nothing back. In her days on the New Orleans police force, she would have been reprimanded and put on a crap shift—if not fired altogether—if she'd discussed a case so openly with a civilian.

Hell, that was precisely why she'd ended up quitting. One too many reprimands for discussing a death designated as storm related with the victim's parents, who'd suspected murder. Either the FBI operated on a different set of rules or Michael thought, as a potential victim, she deserved to know the whole truth.

Either way, she appreciated having the information,

uncensored and unrestrained. Even if she couldn't solve this crime, knowing all the details took the edge off. Her skin felt itchy, her insides hollow from the vulnerability of knowing that some sick bastard had selected her to be his next victim and that he'd been watching her for the past few weeks, if not longer.

She'd never admit her anxiety to Michael. She was having a damned hard time admitting it to herself.

When they reached the cemetery, Claire wasn't entirely surprised to see a parade of mourners congregating near the entrance. Four men in white shirts and black pants held brass instruments while a good dozen other men in suits and ties unloaded a coffin from the back of a hearse. Women in colorful dresses and hats waved paper fans and handkerchiefs, some crying, most talking loudly and jiggling their bodies as if they couldn't wait to dance.

Jazz funerals happened all the time in New Orleans, but Claire's insides turned to stone. What if the boisterous music and grieving crowd scared Josslyn away?

Michael pulled up beside a dark sedan a safe distance from the mourners. The moment he parked, a black woman Claire immediately recognized as FBI stepped out of the car. Her hair was pulled back in a bun made even more severe by the fact that hair of her texture wasn't supposed to be yanked like that. She wore mirrored sunglasses and a navy suit that boxed what Claire suspected might be a curvy figure. She wasn't exactly a standard-issue agent, judging by her bright pink lipstick and diamond-studded earrings—two in each ear.

Michael rolled down his window and his partner leaned in and gave Claire a brazen once-over.

"Ms. Lécuyer, I presume."

Claire smiled. She sensed the agent's territorialism,

but couldn't blame her. On account of Claire, Michael had bent quite a few agency regulations. If his superiors found out how he'd used his brother's money to buy his way into *Nouvelle Placage,* they would not be happy. This couldn't be good news to the guy's partner.

"Special Agent Dawson?" she asked, holding out her hand.

"Ruby," she offered, then shook firmly with Claire. "No sign of your Mother of the Year candidate yet," Ruby quipped.

Clearly, Michael had sent his partner ahead to do reconnaissance, which made Claire wonder why he'd given her such a hard time about coming here in the first place. She shot a questioning look in his direction, but he batted it away with a shrug and a smile.

"Any other entrances to this place?" Michael asked Ruby.

"Only one, and it leads straight out to the main highway. It'd be easier for her to get in and out there."

"I told her the South entrance," Claire said. "But maybe the funeral freaked her out."

She checked the time on the car's console, having given her cell phone to her aunt. Josslyn should be arriving any minute—if she wasn't here already. The funeral goers had started their procession with the band playing a jazz tune that was somewhere in between mournful and exuberant. A half dozen men had hefted the coffin onto their shoulders and the line of mourners behind them popped open a rainbow of parasols to protect themselves from the increasing heat as they followed the family to the gravesite.

"We should get out," Claire suggested. "So she'll see we're here."

Michael grabbed her arm. "I don't want you out in the open."

She rolled her eyes. "He's trying to kidnap me, not shoot me in the head from the other side of a grassy knoll. Relax, Murrieta. You remembered to bring a pen this time, right?"

He released her and shrugged. "This is your party, Ms. Lécuyer. I was assuming you'd thought to bring the writing implement."

From the pocket of her jeans, she retrieved a cheap stick-ballpoint that she'd swiped from the motel. It had the logo of an insurance company etched into the side. She'd even tested it to make sure it worked. This time, she wasn't messing around.

Fifteen minutes went by, and the strains from the jazz funeral could hardly be heard. The tunes now competed with the sounds of traffic passing on the well traveled road. Claire had lifted herself up onto the hood of Michael's rental while the two special agents conferred in whispered tones.

Where was Josslyn? It was now almost eleven thirty, and while Claire had no illusions that the woman valued punctuality, she didn't think she'd totally blow them off. Josslyn wanted a clean break from her old life. She didn't care about having custody of her kids. Claire had not sensed even a glimmer of regret in the woman's attitude last night—more like resignation to the fact that she sucked as a mother and everyone would be better off if she scurried back into the darkness as soon as possible.

The conversation picked up between Michael and Ruby when a call rang through on Michael's cell. He spoke for a minute into the receiver, his back to the noisy road, then quickly crunched over the gravel parking area and held the phone out to her.

"It's your aunt," he said.

Confused, she took the phone. "Clarice?"

"Oh, thank God, you really are there," her aunt said with a huge sigh of relief.

"Why wouldn't I be?"

"I don't know. I'm not used to all this intrigue and danger being real. I much prefer the scripts I read."

Claire slid off the hood of the car and took a few steps away from Michael, hoping for some privacy. Her hope died a quick death. He shadowed her, leaving less than two feet between them. When he said he was sticking with her, he clearly wasn't exaggerating.

"What's wrong, Clarice?" Claire asked. She'd called her aunt last night after they'd left *Nouvelle Placage* and again first thing this morning, using Michael's phone when he'd gone into the bathroom to shave. Her father's sister had nerves of steel and did not fluster easily. "I told you we'll be heading back to the city once I meet with my client's ex."

"I know, but that's just it. She's not coming."

"What? How do you know?"

"Someone called your phone. Some man said that you might as well head home because Josslyn Granger wasn't going to be able to sign anything today."

The alarm on her face must have shown because Michael took the phone from her and started questioning her aunt himself. Her first instinct was to grab his arm, but she was thwarted by Special Agent Dawson's firm grip on her shoulder.

"Just relax," she said, her voice soft, but unyielding. "Michael knows how to ask questions."

"But he doesn't know my aunt."

"Doesn't he?" Ruby asked, smiling slyly. "He convinced her to let you go into some private bedroom with him last night, and I'm guessing that was no easy task."

If Special Agent Dawson expected Claire to look away in embarrassment, then she was sorely mistaken.

"What's that supposed to mean?"

"Back down, buttercup. I'm not judging you. I'm just reminding you that your aunt was supposed to make sure you didn't go upstairs with *anyone,* but Michael is incredibly persuasive. And he's good at what he does."

Claire listened intently, trying to pick up snippets of Michael's end of the conversation. His steady tone soothed her nerves. His short, pointed questions resulted in a phone call that lasted no more than three minutes and ended with Michael handing the phone to Ruby despite Claire's objections.

"Stay on the line with her, Ruby, but get on the road and drive out to her place. Use your own phone to let the local office know I want immediate surveillance until we can move her to a safe location."

"Move her? Safe? What's going on? I want to talk to her," Claire insisted, but Michael had already shuttled her aside and Ruby wasted no time in doing what he'd asked.

"Your aunt will be fine," he said, though she couldn't imagine how he could make such a claim when he'd just sent an FBI detail to her house.

"Then why does she need protection?"

"The man who called your cell phone said something very odd before he hung up. I'm not taking any chances with her safety."

Claire yanked her arm out of his hand. "What did the bastard say? Tell me."

But despite her demand, he didn't answer her question

until Ruby had pealed out of the parking lot and he'd pulled and checked his weapon. "He said Josslyn was busy, only he pronounced the word oddly. Like this—bizz-ee. And he repeated it that way. Twice."

"How else do you say *busy?*"

Michael had her arm again. This time, he propelled her into the cemetery and she decided not to fight. He didn't strike her as someone who would waste time or follow leads that weren't important. Even with dark glasses shielding his eyes, she could tell that he was scanning the area with precision, hesitating only a moment before deciding to go immediately to the right, in the opposite direction of the jazz funeral parade.

"He emphasized the *i* sound and drew out the *z,*" Michael explained.

"Maybe he has an accent."

He continued running up and down the rows of above-the-ground crypts and vaults, stopping when he caught sight of something fluttering across from them. "Or maybe, he was sending us a message."

As they approached the mausoleum, Claire stumbled as if someone had slammed a two-by-four across the back of her knees. In front of a monument to the Bizzey family—the last recorded death being 1876, the year after Paulette began her affair with Joaquin—was a vase filled with fresh-cut, blood-red roses.

And fluttering around the base was a black silk scarf emblazoned with the letter *Z*.

11

ONCE AGAIN, THE sticky heat of the New Orleans night caught him unaware. He traveled around the country for his job all the time, but the first couple of days away from San Francisco always made him a little nostalgic for the chilled nights and fog. He inhaled deeply, amazed at the sweet, sultry scents of this part of the city—so different from the French Quarter where Claire lived and worked or the swampy marshland where they had first met.

Even out of sight, she was never out of mind. Not because their cases had now irrevocably intersected, but because she'd somehow wound her way into his soul.

The tiny courtyard in between the cottage door and the back gate was about the size of the yard outside his condo. In other words, it was only about a fourteen by fourteen foot square of lush grass and fragrant vines that clung to the brick wall separating this former servant's quarters from the grander property next door. With the mossy branches of a live oak hovering above, the sky was nothing more than the occasional swatch of darkening blue. He suddenly wished he smoked so he had a reason to be standing outside, away from Claire, thinking about anything else but her.

And the case—one that was dead in the water until the Bandit made contact. Michael glanced down at his father's ring and resisted the urge to slam it against the stone wall. Was the damned thing working? He needed a strong dose of inspiration right now and the ring wasn't giving him squat.

Behind him, Claire's shadow flitted by the kitchen window. When he'd left her ten minutes ago to check the perimeter, she'd been methodically opening and closing the cabinets, pantry and refrigerator. She'd said she was hungry. That she'd throw something together for dinner.

But Michael knew better. He and Ruby, whom he'd embedded inside the house, might get something to eat in the end, but cooking instead of ordering in was just a way for Claire to expend energy while she figured out how to ask him for one more thing he couldn't provide.

Immediately after the phone call from the Bandit, she'd wanted to see her aunt. He'd denied the request, opting instead to spirit Clarice to relatives in Houston, accompanied by an agent from the New Orleans office. If the Bandit knew to call Clarice, he could also use her as leverage against Claire.

Then Claire had asked to go with him back to *Nouvelle Placage,* to make sure Josslyn was really missing, and if not, to search through her things for any clue about where she might have gone. Instead, he'd ordered her into protective custody and had her brought here. The Bandit had known about their meeting with Josslyn. Either he had some connection to the woman or he'd eavesdropped on their conversation in the secret garden.

For all the security at *Nouvelle Placage,* the fetishists' system had not been perfect. Michael had gotten in. So had Claire. The Bandit could have been anyone from a guest to a bartender or a waiter.

So, until Michael knew what he was up against, Claire would remain in hiding. Whether she liked it or not.

And she definitely didn't like it.

"You done beating yourself up yet?"

Ruby came through the back door, shutting it tight behind her.

"Where's Claire?"

"Whipping you up a Spanish-style tortilla that's going to make you wish you'd grown up in Madrid like that *muy caliente* brother of yours." Ruby came down the steps, rubbing her belly. "Woman has mad kitchen skills. But then, she's from New Orleans. The ability to make great food is a prerequisite for residency, you know."

He hardly cracked a grin. He wasn't in the mood for Ruby's joking around, even if she was only trying to alleviate the tension that was as thick in this safe house as the New Orleans humidity.

"Shouldn't you stay inside with her?"

"So you can mope around here all on your lonesome? She'll be fine for five minutes, Michael. The place is surrounded and I gave her my gun."

He opened his mouth to object, but shut it again, knowing it was no use in challenging Ruby when she was every bit as stubborn as Claire.

"What did you learn at the plantation house?" she asked.

"Nothing useful."

"What about the cemetery caretaker? Anything more from him?"

Michael cursed. He'd allowed himself a split second of excitement when he'd been informed that a worker at St. Honoria's cemetery had reported seeing a strange

character just before Josslyn had been taken, but the eye-
witness account, while useful, hadn't brought them any
closer to finding the Bandit or verifying that Josslyn had
been kidnapped rather than willingly absconded.

"He said he saw a tall guy dressed in a black suit car-
rying roses around the tombs. Figured him for a family
member paying his respects."

"He couldn't describe him?"

"He wore reflective shades that might as well have
been a mask. The agents also interviewed one of the
people from the funeral. She said she saw the dark-suited
man talking to a woman who fit Josslyn's description—
he drove away with her in her car. Best we can figure, it
was about fifteen minutes before we arrived. It doesn't
make sense that she'd take off with a stranger."

Ruby snorted. "You think a woman who fucks men—
two at a time, from what Claire told me—is overly cautious about her safety?"

"But that's the thing," Michael said. "These sexual
fetishists aren't indiscriminate. Most of them don't get
involved unless there are background checks and 'safe'
words. Getting into *Nouvelle Placage* wasn't easy."

"But it wasn't impossible," Ruby reminded him. "This
guy is smart. He obviously found a way to make Josslyn
trust him. I just hope she doesn't pay for that trust with
her life."

Michael's phone buzzed and the second he answered,
Claire appeared on the porch. Instantly, Ruby sprang into
action, shuttling her back inside with Michael tight on
their heels.

Claire ground to a halt right inside the doorway, her
jade eyes wide and worried. Knowing she would dog
him mercilessly until he told her every detail, he hit the

speaker function on his phone and held it out so that both Ruby and Claire could hear the report.

"Can you repeat that?" he asked.

"The next door neighbor received a delivery of red roses for Ms. Lécuyer three hours ago," the agent reported. "They're from a florist shop two blocks away."

"Who sent them?"

"A woman who meets your kidnap victim's description. She paid cash."

"Note?" Michael asked, nearly covering the mouthpiece when Claire blurted out the same question.

"No message. She told the clerk that Ms. Lécuyer would know what they meant and then she left. There was a man with her, but he waited by the door and didn't talk to anyone in the shop."

"Surveillance footage?" he asked, his sharp stare keeping Claire from speaking again. It was bad enough he was sharing investigative information with her—he didn't need the whole of the FBI to know how many rules he'd broken for her.

"We have it, but he's wearing sunglasses and a fedora. We're breaking down the video to see if we can enhance any images or reflections, but so far, nothing. Your missing woman doesn't seem to be in danger, though."

"Looks can be deceiving," he warned. "Keep on it. This is the Bandit we're talking about. All women anywhere near him are in danger."

He disconnected the call. As usual, Ruby's face was impassive, but Claire chewed on her bottom lip, her eyelashes fluttering as she processed all she'd heard.

"At least she's alive," Claire concluded.

"Yes," he replied, keeping the second question, *but for how long?* to himself.

"I want to interview the florist."

Claire stepped closer into a swath of light from a single-bulb fixture that hung above a small table set for one. Her eyes were glossy, but not red. Dark circles marred her flawless coffee-and-cream complexion and her lips, so round and inviting, were chapped from endless gnawing. For a split second, she allowed him to see the full depth of her vulnerability—her guilt, her fear, her self-recrimination. He wanted to pull her into his arms and thaw her icy terror with his body heat, but he didn't dare.

Not here.

Not now.

Perhaps, not ever again.

Despite Ruby's disapproving glare, Michael laid his palm over Claire's. Her warmth seeped into his system like a drug, igniting his nerve endings and accelerating his heartbeat so that he was afraid he might lose his composure and pull her into his arms.

Instead, he moved to the kitchen counter and poured himself a cup of strong black coffee. "Our agents know how to interview witnesses."

"There's only one florist shop close to my house. Annette's. I know her. She might tell me something she wouldn't tell cops or agents."

He shook his head. "There's no reason for the florist not to be forthcoming. If there's anything more to discover, it's on the security video."

"I want to see it."

"You're not leaving this safe house."

"But what if Josslyn tried to send a hidden message in her body language or her mannerisms? I've met her. I know all about her. I might be able to spot something—"

"No," he said.

Claire paced in a tight square. Ruby left the tiny

kitchen, settling back into her spot on the living room couch. The cottage didn't afford much privacy, but Michael considered this a good thing. With Ruby there as chaperone, he found it easier to stay in FBI mode and assuage his guilt over how deeply this was tearing Claire apart.

"Why is she obeying him?" Claire asked. "She's not the kind of woman who follows men's orders."

Something the two of them had in common.

"Maybe he threatened her," he ventured. "Maybe he'd found her long before last night and gained her trust before we showed up. I can come up with a million scenarios, Claire, and none of them are good. No matter how or why Josslyn is involved, she's in danger. And I won't let that happen to you, too."

"What if I don't want your protection?"

"You'll have it anyway."

"Then maybe I'll leave," she shot back. "I'm not under arrest. I didn't ask for your protection. You can't keep me prisoner."

Michael closed his eyes and prayed for calm. "No, I can't. But you're not a stupid woman, Claire. You know you can't go off half-cocked with this guy. He knows you. He'll be counting on you doing what's right rather than what's wise. If you do like you always do, you'll fall right into his hands."

It took a few beats before she realized what he'd said. Yeah, he'd studied her file before coming to New Orleans. That was no secret. But they'd never discussed why she'd left the force or why she'd opted for the private sector, where no one told her what to do. He knew without her telling him—and this did not please her one bit.

Just as he'd done with the book about his notorious

ancestor, Michael had mined Claire's dossier for bits and pieces about her—the kind of revealing nuggets that people in relationships confessed over time. He'd bypassed yet another step toward intimacy, just like he had behind the screen and in the garden.

But this time, Claire didn't get anything good out of it except the baring of a painful memory to a man she hadn't had a chance to really trust.

Michael wandered over to the stove. A cutting board piled with little mounds of onion, garlic and chopped sausage sat on the counter. The scent of spices clung in the air so that his stomach growled.

Claire groaned, then pushed past him and grabbed a metal bowl. She cracked four eggs and started whipping them with the kind of violence she might be imagining she could use on his brains, if she had a chance.

"You don't have to cook for me," he said.

She barked a laugh and pointed her eggy fork at him menacingly. "I'll either cook for you or kill you. Which do you choose?"

He sat down at the kitchen table and unfolded a paper napkin onto his lap.

She turned back to her work. "So how long do you plan to keep me here?"

"Just until we get a clear picture of what the unsub wants."

"He wants me," she said, her tone flat.

"Well, that's the one thing he can't have. He'll contact you, eventually."

"Like with the flowers? The ones without a note?"

"As he grows more desperate to find you, he may try calling again."

"And you have someone at my house and monitoring my phone?"

He didn't bother to answer such an obvious question, but her frustrated sigh sounded more like a growl.

"What is he waiting for? I get it that the flowers are part of his sick seduction, but why doesn't he just call and tell me what he wants? It's been twelve hours since he took her from the cemetery."

Eleven, but who was counting? Michael opened his mouth, prepared to discuss his theories and suppositions with her, but he stopped himself. He'd already told her more than he should. She wasn't his partner. She wasn't even in law enforcement. She was just the woman he was supposed to protect. Nothing more.

She could not be anything more. Not until this mess was settled.

And perhaps, not even then. Especially not if Josslyn was raped or died because he hadn't anticipated her involvement.

"You can't worry about her right now, Claire. Worry about yourself."

"Why do I need to worry about me? I'm incarcerated by the goddamned FBI." The sizzle of vegetables hitting the hot oil in the pan forced her to raise her voice. That and the fact that she was totally pissed off. "She's out there with a madman and no one is looking for her."

"We are looking, but the evidence that she's been kidnapped is circumstantial at best. She's an adult prone to disappearing without a trace. She acted seemingly of her own accord at the florist shop and no one at *Nouvelle Placage* is willing to file a missing person's complaint."

"I'll file the damned complaint!" she insisted. "She was supposed to meet with me and she didn't show."

"The cops know all that, Claire. They're on the lookout for her. But until our unsub makes a move, there's not much we can do."

With a vehement curse, Claire turned to her cutting board and proceeded to hack at the sausage, which he was pretty sure would be nothing but mush soon. For a moment, he allowed himself to be envious of her. As a private investigator, she wasn't bound by laws or procedures or dictates from superiors. If not for him, she could do whatever she wanted, within the confines of the law. And sometimes, she could even skirt that.

But Michael didn't have that freedom. Even his father's ring, glinting at him with mocking brightness, couldn't give him carte blanche to go off half-cocked and put Josslyn in more danger than she might already be in.

The only advantage they had at this point was that the Bandit might not know that a federal agency was on his trail. Michael had ordered the agents working with him to be discreet. Even the interview at the florist shop had been conducted by a female agent dressed casually, as if she'd only gone into the store to order flowers. Michael was keenly aware that if the unsub got spooked, he might kill Josslyn, dump her where they'd never find her and then move on to another victim—another woman distantly related to one of Joaquin Murrieta's lovers.

And then, later, when Michael wasn't here to protect her, the Bandit would come back for Claire.

Unlike the serial criminals he'd chased for years, this unsub wasn't programmed into a single modus operandi. Any part of his ritual that put his seductions at risk would be discarded. And if he stopped sending scarves, they might not find him again until it was too late.

After what seemed like an endless silence, broken only by the scrapes and clanks of cooking, Claire slid a pan sized, inch-thick omelet onto his plate. The aroma of egg, potato, onions, peas and chorizo steamed enticingly beneath his nose and he wasted no time in taking a large and ravenous bite.

"This is good," he said.

"It's comfort food. The freezer was nicely stocked and Ruby arranged for some staples."

He gestured for her to sit across from him, and since she hadn't made any food for herself, he cut off a chunk of his tortilla with his fork and aimed it in her direction.

She waved it away.

He frowned, but didn't push her. He'd bossed her around more than enough today. She'd eat when she was hungry.

"You could be comfortable here," he said.

"Don't you mean *we?*"

He chewed and swallowed the bite she'd refused. "Neither one of us will be here long, Claire. No one wants this to drag out. No one wants Josslyn to get hurt. No one wants you to get hurt."

Least of all, me.

"It's too late for that," she shot back. "And you know it."

THE POWERFUL SCENT of the tortilla stirred the emptiness in Claire's stomach, but she couldn't bear the thought of eating. How could she when Josslyn was missing? The woman might not be a great mother or a responsible wife, but she did not deserve to be held against her will and possibly abused.

No one deserved that.

No one.

She would have to force her worn-out body into remaining upright long enough to help find Josslyn. Her cell phone, retrieved from her aunt and now sitting in front of Ruby, had not rung. No texts. No nothing.

With his silence, the Bandit was killing Claire.

Was that his intention?

"How did he even know about her? About *Nouvelle Placage?*" she asked, needing to force her thoughts in another direction. His mental cruelty would only affect her if she allowed it to.

"Listening device aimed at your office? Tap on your phone? Hack of your email? The possibilities are endless."

"Josslyn didn't arrive in New Orleans until the day before yesterday. That's not enough time for him to have ingratiated himself enough that she'd tell him about our arrangment to meet at the cemetery. She specifically said she didn't want anyone from Nouvelle Placage to know about her past."

He nodded. He hadn't worked that out so succinctly himself. She'd come up with a strong argument against the theory that Josslyn was cooperating with the Bandit willingly. Not that it mattered. Accomplice or not, the woman was at risk as long as she was in the man's company.

"So if she didn't tell him, how did he know about the meeting at the cemetery? No one else was around."

"We don't *think* anyone else was around. We can't be sure."

We were distracted.

He didn't say the words out loud—he didn't need to. She knew as well as he did that they'd been so caught up in each other, they had not sufficiently scoped out the area around the secret garden.

In other words, they'd screwed up.

And Josslyn was going to pay the price.

"We have to find her," Claire insisted.

"We will."

"When? You know that in kidnappings, time is the

enemy. We can't wait around for him to contact us. We have to lure him out. I have to lure him out."

Michael finished his omelet, washed it down with coffee and met her gaze straight on. With his shoulders squared and his jaw tight, he looked implacable.

Infallible.

But he wasn't—and neither was she.

"As we speak, I have agents scoping out positions around your house, sweeping for listening devices inside and reprogramming another cell phone with your number so we can better triangulate calls made to it. The only advantage we have is that there's a small possibility that the Bandit doesn't know that I'm FBI. Until he snatched Josslyn, we were a half step ahead of him. We have to use that advantage."

"And what the hell am I supposed to do in the meantime?"

"Eat," he said, leaning across the counter and retrieving her plate. "Then get some rest. You're going to need it."

"I can't," she said, looking down at the plate as if the egg and potato mixture was crawling with maggots, when, in fact, the scent of chorizo and onion tantalized her tastebuds into watering.

He picked up the plate. She might have resisted, but he speared a chunk of potato and egg onto her fork and waved it under her nose. She'd made this dish about a thousand times over the course of her life and knew how delicious, rich and comforting it was. She took the bite, chewed and swallowed.

Despite her frown, he had another bite ready.

"You don't need to feed me," she protested.

He raised an eyebrow. "Eat."

She did as he asked, and when her hunger took over,

she retrieved the fork from him and finished off the meal on her own. She should have drawn the line at letting him hold the water bottle up to her mouth, but she didn't.

On orders from the agents outside to keep the house dim, she'd cooked with only the light above the stove and the occasional flash from the open refrigerator. The semidarkness had been annoying at the time, but now it rendered the room intimate. When her lips met the rigid edge of the water bottle, she closed her eyes and sipped.

As soon as she swallowed, he kissed her. The sensation was not unlike a puff of warm air, gone before her lids fluttered open and her eyes read the regret on his face. Kissing her, touching her, wanting her when they were in a different world—a make-believe world—was one thing. But doing it here, now, in the presence of his colleagues and in the midst of a major screw up was both technically against the rules and ethically unwise.

So why did she feel so instantly pissed off that he'd stopped?

"I've had enough," she said when he moved to stab another piece of food with the fork. "I'm going to bed."

She didn't give him a chance to argue. She marched out of the kitchen and said good-night to Ruby without breaking her stride. The little bedroom they'd assigned to her, the one that had seemed so tiny when she'd first dumped her stuff onto the twin bed earlier, now echoed with the click from her firmly shut door.

The emptiness only lasted a second. Even before she'd completely turned around, she felt a presence behind her. She swung her fist around, hammerlike, toward the intruder, but he caught her wrist in a powerful grip and smacked his hand tight over her mouth.

"Don't scream."

12

MICHAEL STOOD IN the kitchen, twisting the ring on his finger, when a spike of electricity seared up his spine. His brain registered the sound of a muffled scream, kicking his body into a sprint across the cottage. He kicked open Claire's door, gun drawn.

Somewhere behind him, Ruby shouted, but he wasn't fully aware of anything except Claire's wide green eyes and the male hand clamped over her mouth.

One that immediately released her, then joined the other in high surrender.

"Hey, now everyone calm down here. I'm not your big bad kidnapper."

Michael's eyes refocused from the center of the man's forehead so he could take in the whole face. A familiar face. Dark, like his father's. Like Alejandro's. A couple of days' stubble softened his square jaw, but his eyes gave him away. Bright green and alight with humor, even with two weapons pointed in his direction, thanks to Ruby, who now stood directly to his right.

Danny Burnett, Michael's middle brother, managed a roguish grin.

Almost in unison, Michael and Ruby said, "You!"

Michael dropped his weapon.

Ruby did not.

Danny had the sense to leave his hands in the air—which might have been a bad choice when Claire spun around and coldcocked him directly on the chin.

While she winced in pain, Michael's brother staggered, but remained standing.

"How the hell did you get in here?" Michael snapped.

Claire cursed, shaking her hand. "Who is he?"

"No one dangerous," Michael groused, shoving his firearm into its holster. "Not unless you have something valuable around here you'd like to keep in your possession."

"My life isn't valuable enough?"

"I wasn't going to hurt you," Danny insisted, making quite the show of rubbing his jaw. A trickle of blood marred his lip. When he caught the flash of red on his thumb, he'd seemed impressed. "Probably couldn't have even if I wanted to. That's one hell of a right hook you've got there, sweetheart."

She charged forward, but Michael caught her around the elbow. He wasn't sure why his brother was here—or even if it was legal. Thanks to Alejandro, the trumped up murder charges against Danny had been dropped. While Michael had a few niggling doubts about his brother's innocence, which had been verified in a jailhouse confession by one of the men who'd conspired to set him up, he was fairly certain Danny was still facing a theft charge and had been ordered not to leave California.

"Don't bother bruising your knuckles on him, Claire. He's no threat to you."

"How the hell do you know?"

She'd been pissed off before she'd left the kitchen and Danny's unexpected appearance in her bedroom had her adrenaline pumping so hard, he could practically smell it oozing out of her skin.

The scent was hypnotic and erotic. It took every ounce of his professionalism to keep from dragging her close and inhaling deeply.

"Claire Lécuyer, please meet Daniel Murrieta Burnett. My brother."

Though his jaw was red and swollen, Danny smiled and politely extended his hand. "The pleasure's all mine."

No, the pleasure's all mine. Michael bit back the territorial growl. The way things stood between him and Claire right now, neither one of them was going to experience any type of pleasure in the near future. Not until she no longer needed his protection.

And judging by her deepening scowl in his direction, not after that, either.

Michael turned toward Ruby. She still had her gun drawn, though admittedly, she'd lowered her aim. A shot from her gun right now might not kill Danny, but it would sure as hell hit him where it counted.

"You followed me," she said, grinding her words through tight teeth.

"Sorry," Danny said, though Michael didn't think he sounded the least bit repentant.

Apparently, neither did Ruby. She raised her gun barrel so that she now had a straight shot at his torso.

"I don't like being lied to."

"And believe it or not, I don't like lying. It's an occupational must, of course, but it's not my favorite past time, especially when I'm sharing a drink and oysters with a smoking-hot babe who could probably maim me with her little finger."

Danny hooked his pinky, wiggling the digit until Ruby's

chin quivered with the strain of containing a grin. Michael rolled his eyes. Women found this act charming? Really?

Apparently so, because a split second later, Ruby holstered her gun. "You could have just asked me where your brother was."

"And you would have told me?"

"No," Ruby said. "At the time, I didn't know. And besides, you're a criminal and we don't need you poking around in our case."

"Which is why I opted to don a disguise and follow you from San Francisco until your paths converged. The fact that I'm a criminal is precisely why you need me. Who better to help you catch this joker?"

Michael had not thought it possible to dislike Danny any more than he had the first time they'd met. He was wrong. His blood seethed and it took every ounce of self-control not to use Claire's method of dealing with his brother—though he'd probably aim a little more to the left so he could break his nose.

"We've solved a fair share of cases without your involvement, Daniel. I don't need your help."

"You let Alex front you the money to get into that sex club, but you won't let me contribute my personal expertise to your case?"

"You're a thief," he tossed back. "You steal things. I don't see how your expertise is of any relevance to our situation."

"Well, if what I overheard is correct," Danny said, "you had someone stolen out from under you. I don't usually deal with human contraband, but the principles are the same. The guy has something you want, and with my help, you can steal her back."

CLAIRE CURLED INTO a chair in the cottage's tiny sitting room, an ice pack on her hand while she glanced back and forth between Michael and Danny, trying to figure out how these two men could possibly be related.

Physically, they couldn't be more different. Though Danny had apparently dyed his hair a couple of shades lighter than Michael's as part of his disguise, she could tell from his unshaven face that he was naturally a lot darker. They were about the same height, she supposed, but where Michael was like a stone wall, imposing and insurmountable, Danny was agile and smooth. If she hadn't already learned that he was an internationally re-nowned thief, she might have pegged him for a dancer.

Not ballet or a Twyla Tharp-type. He was like Gene Kelly or Fred Astaire. Old school.

Suave—and more than a little full of himself.

Michael, on the other hand, was deceptive. In FBI mode, he was serious and driven. He possessed a single-minded focus that never wavered, despite the residual sensuality of the man he'd portrayed at the plantation, the man who'd made love to her so wildly in the shower, the man who'd stolen a sweet and secret kiss in the kitchen when he'd known she was frustrated and angry at the impotence of her situation.

Danny wore his personality all over his body, but Michael—Michael was a man with two faces. And she yearned for both of them and neither at the same time.

Bottom line? Michael Murrieta and Daniel Burnett had absolutely nothing in common, except for their dual ability to totally piss her off.

Danny continued to manipulate his jaw, as if checking to see if she'd done any permanent damage. Her hand numb, she silently offered him the ice pack Ruby had fetched from the freezer.

He waved it away. "No, thank you, darling. I'll wear this bruise like a badge of honor. There's nothing more valuable to a guy like me than being knocked down a peg by a beautiful woman."

Yeah, he was a charmer.

Michael, standing sentry in the middle of the room, groaned. Ruby, who had not stopped glowering at Danny from the doorway, remained deathly quiet.

"If you don't need medical attention, then why don't you clear out?" Michael asked.

"You think I traveled all this way to be sidetracked by a love tap to the chin?"

Claire sat up straighter, but Danny winked at her. He was just using her to bait his brother.

The least she could do for Michael was not fall for it.

"So why did you come here?" she asked.

"My area of expertise is unique. Why not use it to outsmart your...what's that word you FBI guys use... your unsub? Or do you prefer the Bandit."

"Unsub will do," Michael snapped. "But I fail to see how the tricks of the thievery trade will help us deal with a man who kidnaps women for kicks."

"He's not doing it for kicks," Danny replied. "He takes the women to fulfill a fantasy—a fantasy based on our ancestry. But whatever his reasons, the fact remains— he's a thief. Instead of focusing on baubles and trinkets, he steals women. And a thief is a thief. And you know the saying, *set a thief to catch a thief.*"

Claire glanced at Michael, who was staring up at the ceiling as if pleading with God for help, or patience, or a little of both. Ordinarily, Claire would have thought Danny's reasoning a stretch at best, but with no leads, they could at least hear him out. Ruby, still pissed off that she'd been tailed by Michael's ne'er-do-well brother without her knowledge, remained silent and sullen. Michael was probably battling with too many demons—old and new, personal and professional—to make a judgment call.

It was up to her.

"Okay, then what's your take on the situation?" she asked.

Michael shot her a warning glare, but she ignored him. At this point, she was willing to listen to the garbage man assigned to her street if it meant coming up with a plan for rescuing Josslyn that didn't include sitting around and waiting.

Danny rewarded her with a smile that was probably worth as much as some of the jewels he'd stolen. "I'm glad you asked. Strip away the black scarves and sicko seductions, and you still have a man who is taking things that don't belong to him."

"How do you know about the scarves?" Ruby asked.

"As much as he'd like to deny it, Michael has two brothers, Special Agent Dawson. He shared with Alejandro and Alejandro—"

"Shared with you?" Michael asked, incredulous. "He may have saved your ass from a trumped up murder rap, but he would not tell you about my case."

Danny's mouth curved into an expression that was halfway between a regretful frown and an admiring smile. "True, but he also doesn't pay a lot of attention to who might be eavesdropping on his calls. The manner in which I gained my insight notwithstanding, it seems to me that the unsub is, at his heart, a thief. As I said, he's taken something you want and he's holding onto it on his terms. He's throwing you off your game and putting you on the defensive."

He aimed that last insight directly at Michael, who had indeed retreated into protective mode. Claire sat up straighter, realizing that as much as she might not like

Michael's brother's method of entry into their lives—or his chosen profession—she might just have found an ally.

"What do you propose we do, then?"

"Claire." Michael spun, glaring at her.

She stared right back. If he didn't want to have this conversation with his brother, he could see the door from where he was standing. She, on the other hand, wanted to hear what the bad guy had to say.

"I'd play him right back," Danny said, his tone light and jovial, as if he hadn't just cut into a moment so full of tension, it might have snapped. "He's playing you by taking what you wanted—Josslyn. Now you have to take what he wants."

"I have what he wants," Michael said. "I have Claire."

Danny grinned. "Precisely."

"If he wanted to trade Josslyn for me, wouldn't he have contacted us by now and proposed a trade?" Claire asked.

"Not if he doesn't know how to find you. You haven't gone home."

"He has my cell number," she argued. "He can call."

"He's called that number once already. He's not going to take a chance of being traced. He wants a face-to-face. My brother knows it. That's why he's keeping you so tightly under wraps."

Michael, who'd turned again to face Danny, didn't move. He didn't deny Danny's accusation, nor did he acknowledge it. He didn't have to.

"So how do I contact him?" Claire asked.

"Go home."

Michael bolted forward and grabbed his brother by the collar. Danny didn't tense up. He might have been a rag doll for all the resistance he gave. But Claire shot to her feet and demanded Michael release Danny immediately.

"Let him go, Michael, or I swear to God, I'm walking out that door and you won't be able to stop me."

Michael threw his brother back, and though he fumbled a bit when he hit the chair, Danny made quite the show of straightening his dark shirt and pants before sliding back into his seat. "Well, now that we've gotten that out of way, I say we move on to formulating a plan."

"We're not discussing any more of this with you," Michael hissed. "I'm calling Alejandro so he can get you the hell out of here."

Danny laughed, unperturbed. "Damned shame we missed out on sharing our childhoods. No opportunities to tattle on each other. I guess we can blame Ramon for that. Or, what did you call him? Pop?"

Claire watched Michael's shoulders bunch. He clenched his fists and took a menacing step forward.

This time, even Danny flinched.

"Leave him out of this."

Claire darted forward and grabbed Michael's arm. "Stop it," she ordered. "Both of you. The only family relative that matters right now is the one the Bandit is emulating to satisfy his sick fantasies. The rest can wait until after we've rescued Josslyn."

"The lady makes an excellent point," Danny said with a sycophantic tone that made Claire frown. He cleared his throat, sat up straighter and folded his hands as if he'd morphed into, well, into Michael. "Pops isn't the issue. Neither is Alex, who did indeed arrange for my release from jail, but the charges were completely dropped. I'm a free man, no longer tethered to the justice system of

California or any other state. So, let's focus on the matter at hand, shall we?"

Claire ran her hand up Michael's arm, admiring the strength there even as she met his gaze, which was equally determined. She did not know what bad blood existed between the brothers, but right now, one of them was her unexpected collaborator and the other was a man she could love. Couldn't he see that they had to look at every possibility, every scenario, to make the right choice about what to do next?

"Please, Michael. At least hear him out. His idea might be bullshit, but it also might be worth listening to."

She squeezed his bicep even as she slipped her other hand into his. The gesture indicated a greater intimacy than she would have wanted to reveal in any other situation, but the time for pretending was over. For the first time since Josslyn disappeared, Claire had a chance to do something to save her. And if it meant breaking out of Michael's protective shield, that's what she'd do.

But she'd rather do it with his cooperation than without it. She wasn't stupid. At this point, the Bandit did have the advantage against her. But what she had was nearly as potent—an FBI agent who cared about her.

"Sit down, Michael. Please."

He brushed his other hand against hers briefly, then reached for a chair, which he dragged into the center of the room, as if he meant to shield Claire from Danny's presence. Claire opted to remain behind him, her wrists resting on the back of the chair, her fingers dangling just above his shoulders.

"So," Michael snapped. "Speak."

Danny smirked, but did as he was asked. "This Bandit

of yours doesn't play by the traditional rules. You can't profile him with any degree of accuracy because he keeps changing things up. But the one thing that hasn't changed is that he's a criminal. He wants what he's not supposed to have."

Michael cursed under his breath. "You don't get him at all. He believes these women do belong to him. He believes he's entitled to have them—and worse, he believes they want him in return."

Danny leaned forward, breaking into Michael's personal space. "And you're overthinking the situation. It's a simple matter of supply and demand. You have what this Bandit wants. Give it to him."

"Give up Claire?"

Michael moved to stand, but Claire pressed down on his shoulders, keeping him in his chair.

"You're insane."

Danny snickered. "That's beside the point. But no, I don't mean you should literally give up Claire. But dangle her. Tempt him with her. Taunt him out of hiding, then do everything you can to make sure he doesn't snatch her when you're not looking."

Claire turned to Ruby, who'd been sitting in total silence. The whites of her eyes glowed against her dark skin, but her mouth was pursed as if the concept shocked her, but still had merit. Michael, on the other hand, shook with rage. This time when he moved to stand, there was nothing she could do to stop him.

"I won't put Claire in danger. Not for Josslyn Granger. Not for anyone."

Michael stalked out of the cottage, slamming the door behind him. Ruby stared daggers at Danny, but after a reassuring nod from Claire, went after her partner.

Claire crossed her arms and stared at Danny, who

hadn't moved a muscle from his comfortable spot in a cushy armchair.

"Why do you bait him?"

"Isn't that what brothers do?"

"I wouldn't know," Claire answered. "I was an only child."

Danny chuckled humorlessly. "So was I."

At her quizzical stare, he unfolded his legs and leaned forward, elbows on his knees. "We didn't exactly have a traditional family. In fact, our father didn't even know I existed for most of my life. Not that it would have mattered. He fathered another child in Spain—Alejandro—and abandoned him without a backward glance. The only one who grew up with Ramon was Mikey."

"So you traveled all the way across the country to punish your brother because he got to play catch with Daddy and you didn't?"

For the first time since she'd met him, Danny looked ruffled. His brow furrowed, and inside the grim line of his mouth, she could tell he was grinding his teeth.

"I came here to help," he said finally. "My reasoning is sound and you know it."

"But he's a trained FBI special agent with years of experience and probably a list of commendations that match the length of your rap sheet," she countered. "He's not going to listen to you unless you give him sound, logical reasons that can trump what his gut is telling him."

"And his gut is telling him to protect you at all costs—even at the cost of another woman's life?"

Claire rubbed her face, hoping it would cover the flush suffusing her skin.

It didn't.

He whistled long and loud in apparent surprise. "Well,

well. Looks like he really does have Murrieta blood running through his veins. Maybe it's Pop's ring. It's supposed to have magical powers, you know."

"Right," Claire said, settling herself into the chair Michael had just occupied. His lingering warmth cradled her, comforted her. Gave her the strength to look his brother dead in the eye and quip, "Then why haven't you stolen it yet?"

"I've tried, but the woman I sent to snatch it from Alejandro fell in love with him instead. Damned inconvenient. Now Michael has it, and frankly, an FBI agent is a tough guy to steal from. But then I realized, if Michael doesn't totally screw up this…opportunity," he said, briefly looking her up and down in a way that made her cross her arms over her chest. "It will naturally come to me anyway. And just for future reference, my rap sheet is surprisingly short. I rarely get caught."

"I thought you were just in jail."

"I was set up. That's why I'm out."

"Doesn't seem to matter to Michael. He doesn't like you, much less trust you."

"Well," Danny said, leaning back. "He hardly knows me. If he did, he'd totally hate my guts. But he'd also realize that I know what I'm talking about."

"So you think I should just go home and wait for the Bandit to try and catch me?"

He laughed. "You think Mikey would agree to that? Not in a million years. However, we could go one better." He leaned forward and presented his idea in a whisper. "He wants to be your lover, right? Why not trip him up by showing him that you already have one?"

13

WATCHING THE INTIMATE scene from outside the window, Michael experienced a hot streak of fury that felt a hell of lot like a bullet tearing through flesh. If he couldn't stand his own brother getting this close to Claire, how would he ever survive if the Bandit got even within one-hundred feet of her.

He wouldn't.

The realization rocked him. Since he'd first signed on with the Bureau, Michael had never put his own needs above those of ensuring justice. He'd worked twenty-hour days for weeks on end. He'd had no serious relationships and pursued no outside interests except for exercise and defense training, all of which related directly back to his job. He only collected Zorro memorabilia because his father gave it to him—he'd never once trolled an estate sale, flea market or online trading site himself. To avoid conflicts of interest, he kept his friendships contained to fellow agents and had even failed to truly forge a relationship with either of his half brothers because Alex had been too far away and Danny's tarnished reputation might have stained his own sterling one.

But when it came to Claire, he wasn't willing to make

any more sacrifices. He wouldn't dangle her in front of
a potential killer like fresh, bloody meat over a shark's
tank.

Not for the Bureau—and sure as hell not for Danny.

Ruby came up behind him. "If you had lasers in your
eyeballs, your brother would have a hole in his chest
right now."

Michael pushed away from the window. "Give it a
rest, Ruby. I know he pushes my buttons."

"He pushes mine, too," she commiserated. "Doesn't
mean he's not right."

Michael stalked around the small side yard, but Ruby
remained still, waiting as she always did, for him to
burn off his excessive energy and focus in on the heart
of the matter. He didn't want to hear the truth any more
than he wanted to watch Claire cozily scheming with
his brother, but Ruby wouldn't let this go. Not unless he
could come up with a better plan that didn't mean putting Claire in the line of fire.

"Look, you care about her," Ruby said. "I get it. And
I think it's too risky to send her home alone and wait for
the jerk to take her right from under our noses. But the
underlying idea is sound. We just need to flip it around.
She's our ace-in-the-hole. We can't ignore that."

Her keen assessment made him stop his pacing. If
Ruby understood that he couldn't put Claire in danger,
maybe they could work out another way to use her to
catch the Bandit.

"Protocol says we wait for the unsub to contact us
while we're actively pursuing any and all leads to finding him. Truth is, we don't even know for sure that Josslyn didn't go with him willingly. He could have paid her.
Offered him some kinky sex experience she's always
wanted to try."

Ruby strolled closer, her arched eyebrow visible as she came closer. "And what does your gut tell you on that?"

He cursed. He had no proof, but he was one-hundred percent certain that Josslyn had not gone with the unsub on her own. The *Nouvelle Placage* event happened only once a year, and from all of Claire's intel, she hadn't missed a single gathering since she'd left her family to do the sexual deviant circuit. Tonight's ball was the main event, and according to the agent he'd left on the scene, she hadn't shown up.

"He has her," he confessed. "And she's in danger."

"Right," Ruby agreed. "She has no value to him except as a means to lure Claire into the open."

"Then why hasn't he called yet? Tried to arrange for a trade?"

Ruby shook her head. "No idea. Maybe because he doesn't know precisely where Claire is. If he follows his MO, he's had her in his sights for weeks. She's off-grid now and that might have thrown him off his game. We need to let him see her."

Michael opened his mouth to object, but Ruby held up her hand. "I don't mean face-to-face. From a distance. He watched all the women from afar before he finally swooped in and took them. I've got agents making very discreet inquiries about the recent renters in her neighborhood, particularly properties with views of her building. One of them is going to pop as a potential suspect. It just makes sense."

"He could be using electronic surveillance," he argued.

"He could, but that's expensive and lacks the personal, romantic touch he seems so fond of. We're going to get a bead on him sooner rather than later."

"But it might not be soon enough," he said. "Not for Josslyn."

"Nope, not for her."

Michael took a quick turn around the front garden, checking the lock on the gate and wondering how his brother had breached security. The detail he'd assigned to watch the house from the outside remained in place. Except for one glitch, his orders had been followed to the letter. Claire was safe—but at what cost?

He was too close to this—too personally involved. He needed distance, but he wasn't about to stray more than twenty-five feet from Claire. Not until the bastard was caught.

"What do you think we should do?" he asked Ruby.

She frowned. "You're not going to like my answer."

"Tell me anyway."

"We have an advantage with Claire," Ruby said. "She's not just another potential victim. She's not just a woman you've come to care about more than you should, either. She's a former cop. She's a successful private investigator who's managed to keep herself out of trouble even when she's going into dangerous situations."

"The unsub knows all that," Michael argued. "He'll expect her to be tougher to catch. Tougher to subdue. He won't go after her in her house, not when he knows she's armed."

"He hasn't gone after any of the women in their homes. To a one, he strikes when they're out in public."

"So what do we do, parade her at her favorite club?"

Ruby shook her head. "Just the opposite. We need to shut her in and give this guy every reason to think that she's not going out—not alone—anytime soon. He has a deadline, right? Three days after the delivery of the first scarf. Three days is tomorrow. We need to force his hand."

Michael grabbed on to the wrought iron gate, nearly unaware of the grime clinging to the metal or the way the rusty spots bit into his skin. Light from the nearby streetlamp flickered above the branches of the trees shielding the house from above. He had indeed found an ideal place to keep Claire from harm, but in doing so, he'd ground the investigation to a halt. He needed to act. Josslyn's life did matter to him—and more than that, it mattered to Claire.

"So he's been watching her. He delivered the scarf on Thursday morning, which means he fully intended to take her by Sunday. Where does she usually go on Sunday?"

"Church? Visiting family? Maybe she sleeps in. Whatever she usually does, you need to make the unsub think she's not going to do it. That she has a better offer. A reason to stay in, if you know what I mean."

Him.

Danny's words drifted back into his mind. The unsub wanted Claire as a lover. He'd been watching her for months, waiting for the opportunity to make it real. Like the four women he'd taken before, Claire was single and available, but she was also the most highly desirable, descended from the woman Joaquin Murrieta had wanted above all.

What kind of wrench would they throw into the unsub's mind if Claire suddenly showed up at home with a lover? A man who would give her every reason to stay indoors, in bed and out of the Bandit's clutches?

Michael's body instantly reacted to the images suddenly flashing in his brain of him and Claire walking up her street, pawing each other, flaunting their lust, maybe

even ducking into a shadowed corner—in full view of
the many windows lining her street. Then they would
slowly, sensually, make their way to her bedroom, and
with the shades open, show the obsessive unsub exactly
what he couldn't have.

"Claire will have to agree to it," he said, but he knew
before he said it that this would not be an issue. She'd
already proved she was willing to do whatever it took
for a case.

Ruby gave him a fortifying slap on the shoulder.
"Stop looking so put out. The worst thing that happens
is you two burn off a little bit of that massive sexual
tension you have going on. All those pheromones are
playing havoc with my sex deprived body. So unless
you want me to work off my own needs with the closest
single man around—who happens to be your brother—
you'll do this."

"Thanks, Ruby. Talk about motivation."

Ruby laughed. "Hey, a girl's gotta do what a girl's
gotta do."

MICHAEL SHOVED THE gear shift into Park, leaned across
the front seat and kissed Claire as if her life depended
on it.

In this case, the cliché was true. Even now, they were
being watched. Less than an hour ago, his team had finally identified a possible person of interest—a man
who'd rented the third-floor apartment on Claire's French
Quarter street. The place had a fairly clear catty-corner
view of Claire's bedroom, and the man who rented it
had paid cash, came and went during strange hours and
made it a point to never talk to his neighbors. When he
did venture out, he favored an entirely black wardrobe,

giving the feds every reason to believe he was the man they were looking for.

But no proof. And no sign of Josslyn.

If the plan worked, however, the guy might tip his hand and reveal enough evidence to rescue Josslyn and make an arrest for aggravated kidnapping, stalking and rape.

And most importantly, Michael would have the rock solid proof that would keep Claire safe.

He leaned back only enough to break the kiss. She'd swiped on a layer of strawberry-flavored balm, and when he licked his lips, his senses yearned for more.

"You're sure you want to do this?" he asked.

Even in the dark car, he could see Claire's eyes glisten with determination—and to his surprise, desire.

"Why wouldn't I?"

"He'll be watching," Michael reminded her.

"That's the whole point. Besides, we're pretty hot when we think someone's watching."

She moved to open her door, but Michael popped out and ran around to get it for her. Maybe he was taking his vow not to let her out of his presence too far, but he wasn't taking any chances.

Not with Claire.

She slid out of the car, then leaned provocatively against the door so that he couldn't resist pressing his entire body flush against hers and kissing her again. She snaked her hands around his neck and rocked her pelvis against his. If she was teasing him for the benefit of the unsub, he didn't care. The sensations ricocheted through his body and he couldn't resist grabbing her by the ass and pressing her even closer while he kissed her until she could barely breathe.

"You're not playing fair," she murmured.

He slid his hands up her waist, his fingers teasing just along the edges of her T-shirt. "Neither are you."

"Then I guess we're perfect for each other."

She grabbed his hand, barely giving him time to lock the car before she dragged him up the stairs of her porch. There, under the porch light, Claire's tongue tangled with his, making it oh-so-easy to forget that not only the unsub was watching them, but so were Ruby and two other agents he'd posted on Claire's street.

But only Michael had the job of watching Claire from inside. Once they crossed the threshold, the only person privy to what they did in her bedroom would be the suspected Bandit.

Amid laughter and sensual tickling, Claire used her keys to unlock her front door and then pulled him inside. She moved to flip on the lights, but he stayed her hand while he turned her deadbolts and pushed her slide lock into place.

"Not yet," he said. "Stay here."

As hard as it was to force himself back into FBI mode, he left her by the door and did a quick sweep of the interior of the house. Once certain the place was secure, he returned to find her leaning saucily against the door.

"Satisfied?" she asked.

"Not hardly."

She popped open the top button of her jeans and sashayed toward him. "I'm not going to think about the fact that some crazy man might be watching us."

Sliding her hands into his hair, she pulled herself up and placed a feather soft kiss on his lips.

"We can't forget," Michael insisted. "Not for a minute."

"Ruby's outside, right? With your team? They're watching the whole street, including his front and back doors. Even if he wanted to come and join us, he wouldn't make it inside."

On this, she had a point. Before Michael had given the green light to this operation, he'd made sure that the only way the unsub could reach them was via the cell phone Claire carried in her pocket.

Claire jogged up the stairs ahead of him and the view of her round backside burned away any lasting concerns. For this brief moment in time, they were doing precisely what they needed to be doing. For the case. For themselves.

When she rounded the corner into her bedroom, he snagged her by the waist and spun her into his arms. She squealed in surprise, but melted in to him even as he fumbled along the wall to turn on the overhead light.

She tugged at his shirt, made quick work of his buttons and then pushed the material off his shoulders while he attempted to untangle his limbs. The minute he was free, she shoved him gently backward so that he tumbled onto the bed.

He blinked, frozen as she moved directly into the line of sight of the window. Slowly, she drew her T-shirt up, higher and higher, revealing her café mocha skin inch by sensual inch. About mid-way up her torso, she stopped, her eyes darting warily to the side.

"What's wrong?"

She tried to laugh and shake off her sudden hesitation, but she remained still, unmoving.

"Maybe it's my imagination, but it's like I can feel his eyes on me."

"They probably are," he said, scooting forward and bracing his hands on his knees. "We can stop now, Claire. Maybe he's seen enough."

She pulled her cell phone out of her back pocket and tossed it on the bed.

"Not until he calls."

"Then focus on me. I'm watching you, too, and believe me when I tell you that I'm enjoying the show way more than he ever could. I know firsthand how beautiful you are. How free. How giving."

He stood, unbuckled his jeans and dropped them. He watched her eyes widen at the sight of him, naked and vulnerable not only to her, but likely to some freak. When he sat back down, his erection slapped against his thigh. He was hard. Ready. What happened inside this room was between them. Someone else might be watching, but no one else mattered.

"Let my eyes be the only ones you feel."

With quivering slowness, she resumed her removal of her shirt. Inch by fabulous inch, he spied her slim belly, lacy bra, irresistible shoulders. She shook her head, mussing her thick hair and in a burst of playfulness, she tossed her shirt at him.

He clutched it like a lifeline.

Next, she unzipped and shimmied out of her jeans. In nothing but a bra and the same style of pale pink panties she'd worn the night before, she stood before him, all curves and delicious latte skin. When she reached behind her and unhooked her bra, he saw her gaze dart to the window.

"I can't wait to taste you," he said, his voice hoarse and rough with want.

The straps loosened on her shoulders, but she kept her hands beneath the cups, keeping her lovely ladies contained until he thought he might lose his mind.

He crooked his finger. She took a step nearer, striking a pose that emphasized her every intoxicating curve.

Impatient, he snared her by the waist and pulled her onto his lap. The minute her backside pressed against his sex, his body surged with a wave of desire equal to a tsunami. But he held his breath, determined to make this last.

Starting at her shoulders, he placed a trail of kisses along her collarbone to the hollow of her neck. Her skin, so soft and pliant, acted like the strip on the side of a matchbox, igniting and inflaming him so that he couldn't resist running his tongue down until he could slip the tip just inside the lace of her bra. He flicked her erect nipple and the fire spread from him to her. She loosened her grip and the bra melted away.

She tangled her fingers into his hair and tugged. The pain was exquisite and potent, urging him to squeeze her bottom until she arched her back in full offering. He no longer cared whether she'd forgotten the man outside. All he wanted was to taste her, pleasure her, fill her mind with nothing but the crazy, wonderful madness that was pure sexual delight.

She might not remember who was likely spying on them through the window, but he did.

And he wanted that bastard to get one message and one message only: *mine.*

Her cell phone rang.

Instantly, she tensed. He clamped his mouth around her areola and sucked in hard, destroying any thoughts that might be lingering in her brain beyond the very basic, animalistic urge to take what he was offering.

"Michael," she pleaded, but he did not stop. He continued his sensual assault, slipping his hands beneath the barrier of her panties, guiding her legs until they were wrapped around his waist. When her sweet center met

his full erection, his mouth grew hungrier, his teeth unyielding and nearly cruel.

The phone continued to ring.

"Mi—"

"Make him wait," he murmured against her skin,
loving the texture of her moist, puckered nipples beneath his insistent thumbs. "You're not waiting for his
call, sweetheart. You're enjoying the attention of a man
who can't get enough of you."

Michael swung her around, laying her flat on the
bed. The phone stopped trilling for a second, but then
began again. He used the music to gauge his speed as
he dragged her panties down her legs.

He bent down and kissed her breasts again, then her
belly, and then the sinfully scented curve of her pubic
bone, just above the sweet center he intended to taste
very, very soon.

But first, he reached up and yanked the chain on the
light of her ceiling fan. The blades continued to stir the
air in gentle eddies, but the darkness doused the scene
so that no one could see her—no one but him.

"What are you doing?"

He grabbed her cell phone and set the ringer to vibrate.

"He's seen enough."

"But he's calling. That's what we wanted."

He tossed the phone onto a plush armchair tucked in
the corner near her closet, then returned to his position
just above her. His eyes adjusted to the dimness so that
the streetlamps threw enticing shards of light across her
beautiful, nude body.

"He's calling because he's furious. He's watching
another man live out his fantasy, but now we've cut the

lights. He can't see anything. That really has to get under his skin."

"But if I don't pick up—"

"He'll leave a message," he replied, running his hands up her arms until her hands entwined with his. "And my agents will intercept it and trace it. If it's more than a rant, they'll call me. That call I'll answer."

"But if he's so angry, Josslyn—" she argued.

"—is not with him in the apartment," Michael said. He laid his body over hers and locked her hands above her head, effectively keeping her precisely where he needed her to be. "And if he's holding her at another location and we piss him off enough, he'll have to leave to get his revenge. And Ruby will be right behind him."

With that declaration, Michael dismissed the case from his mind. It was wrong. It went against everything he'd ever done, everything he'd ever believed in, but he could not help himself. He'd prepared for every scenario except one—going through the motions of making love to Claire without actually finishing what they'd started. With her writhing so lusciously beneath him, he couldn't imagine any other outcome but pressing deep inside her, sliding in and out of her until she cried out his name in unrestrained ecstasy.

But even as the head of his erection met with her sweet, moistened skin, she squeezed her thighs and denied him entrance.

"What if the guy across the street isn't the Bandit? What if it's someone else? Someone we don't know about."

He tried to contain his impatience, tried to ignore the fact that in any other circumstance or with any other woman, he would have asked the same question.

"And what if you stop enjoying your new lover long

enough to answer an unknown caller? What if that tips him off that what he's been watching isn't real?"

She wasn't entirely convinced, but she relaxed enough so that he knew she wasn't going to bolt. But the moment of need had ebbed. He reached across and retrieved the phone, turning it so that the large LCD screen on the outside showed nothing but two missed calls from an unidentified number. Seconds ticked by and there was no message. No third call.

He tossed the phone aside again.

"See? He's lost interest. But I haven't. If you don't want to do this, that's cool. Now is the time to stop. But I want you, Claire. I've never wanted anyone or anything more than I do right now."

She blinked, as if what he'd confessed surprised her. That confused him. Did she have no idea how powerful she was?

"You're exaggerating."

He took her hand and pressed it against his cock. The moment might have splintered, but blood still rushed through his system like a tidal wave of hot lava.

"Does this feel like an exaggeration?"

"No," she said with a whimper, wrapping her hand completely around him and squeezing tight. "It feels like heaven."

14

CLAIRE TRIED TO resist, tried not to fall under the spell of his hot, silky skin against her hand, tried not to become bewitched by Michael's guttural groans. Not because she didn't want him. Her body yearned for the glorious madness that she'd felt last night in the shower when he'd finally yielded to their undeniable lust and nailed her against the tile. It had been wild and hot—an experience she wouldn't forget anytime soon.

But this? This was better. Even if someone had been watching.

Even if he still was.

Because this was in her bed, in her space, and there wasn't just lust between them anymore. Now, she cared about him.

And though he had not said as much, he'd proved in a hundred little ways how much he cared about her. Every action he'd taken since he'd shown up in her life reflected how he put her needs above everything—even his own job.

The world outside—a world she could barely remember as his lips trailed a tender path down her body—held dangers and conflicts that needed resolution. Josslyn needed to be saved. The Bandit needed to be caught.

Michael trusted his team to get the job done, but he also trusted his instincts. If he believed the two of them should steal this brief, intimate moment, who was she to argue?

So far, trusting him hadn't let her down.

Like a race car filled with jet fuel, their relationship, such that it was, had gone from zero to light speed in a series of rapid-fire explosions that tore at every belief she'd ever had about men and sex.

She didn't trust men, but she trusted Michael.

She loved hot sex, but never above all else—except with Michael.

For him, she'd stop the world. For him, she'd tear away her masks.

He eased her knees apart, slid his arms beneath her legs and blew a hot breath to dance across her skin.

"Oh," she cooed.

He answered with a hum of appreciation before he set to the task of tasting her, touching her, exploring her every intimate cleft until he'd sampled every part of her. She squirmed, but never enough to move out of his reach, crying out in unrestrained pleasure when his tongue parted her labia and he took a long, deep taste and sent her body into a tailspin. She dug her fingernails into his shoulders, needing to hold on while her body rocketed so high, she feared the fall might knock her senseless.

"Michael," she begged, though she wasn't sure what more she wanted. The pleasure coursing through her body was intoxicating. She couldn't think—couldn't feel anything beyond his mouth on her, pleasuring her, filling her with needs she couldn't make sense of, beyond the very basic.

This was sex. This was more than sex. This was ecstasy.

She melted into the mattress, surprised when Michael changed tactics and kissed up her torso, pausing briefly to lave her breasts before he sucked the pulse point in her neck and then her ear, chin and finally, her mouth. The intimate flavors on his lips threw her into a wild hunger she'd feared she would never sate.

"This isn't an act," he whispered.

"What?"

His erection pressed against her, a bold promise of hard, unyielding pleasure.

"Making love to you," he confessed. "I mean every touch, every kiss. It's real. More real than I've ever felt."

Her undulations against his body ceased as the depth of emotion in his words hit her. "I never thought it was fake, Michael. Never for a minute. That's not you."

He kissed her again, this time longer, deeper. "How can you know me? Half the time we've been together, we've been pretending to be people we're not."

Reaching down, she grabbed his buttocks. Wrapping her legs around him, she tugged until he slid deeper inside. The sensations rocked her nearly as much as the tenderness of what he was trying to confess. She'd never felt so cherished, so protected.

So loved.

"That's where you're wrong, Michael. That man who swept me off the dance floor at *Nouvelle Placage* was you. The man who's risked everything since then to protect me is you. The real you. The you that you've probably never shown anyone else. The you that belongs to me. The you I could fall in love with, but won't unless you finish what you've started."

Needing no more encouragement, he pressed fully inside her. Claire's body was consumed with pleasure, but it was her heart that was on the brink of explosion. She'd said the word *love* and he hadn't hesitated, hadn't bolted like so many other people had when she let down her guard and allowed herself to feel something.

Michael not only stayed, he'd joined with her.

With her body.

With her soul.

His tempo was slow, rhythmic and thorough. No matter what might be happening in the outside world, every element in him was focused entirely on her.

"God, I love how you feel," he said.

She hummed her approval, slowly losing herself in the sensations of his body, his skin silkily sliding inside her, filling her with a heat that suffused every nerve ending, every cell. She clutched at him, kissed him, touched him everywhere within reach.

Then speed overtook them. Need pushed them to the edge. His thrusts met hers and in a destruction of seconds, her cries became uninhibited. Powerful.

Loud.

When they were less than a heartbeat away from orgasmic release, he inexplicably stopped.

The pressure of his head was intense. If she moved, they'd both come. But she remained still, frozen, waiting for him to say whatever had forced him still.

"Michael," she whispered, blinking away the sensations that were turning her darkened room into a kaleidoscope of reds, blues and purples.

Above her, his biceps bulged and his skin glistened with sweet, salty sweat. When he opened his mouth to speak, he was panting, half from the exertion of the sex and half, she anticipated, from the weight of what he suddenly wanted to say.

"I care about you, Claire. More than you realize."

She caressed his cheek, her heart nearly cracking in two when he pressed his face into her palm in complete, utter surrender.

"I know, Michael."

"No, you don't. We haven't had enough time together. We've done this all wrong. All backward. I should have—"

She slid her thumb over his mouth and started to move beneath him. She considered trying to flip him over, but knew such a tumble would break their contact. Instead, she writhed and undulated, lifting her bottom until he groaned and relaxed.

"What should you have done, Michael? Sent me red roses? Maybe a pretty scarf? He ruined all those romantic gestures for me. This is much better."

The minute his lips touched hers, the wild ride they'd been on restarted, this time with more vigor, more speed, more intensity than she'd ever thought possible. In seconds, she fell apart. Her skin rippled, as if invisible seams had formed just so they could tear open and free her heated insides.

Then Michael enfolded her with a thousand caresses, a thousand kisses, and with one strong thrust filled her with his essence.

So this is what it felt like to be a woman in love.

The shock of the realization knocked her out of the zone. She heard a foreign sound. A mosquito? A fly? She looked around and saw the LCD screen on her phone flash with a number she could not read from this distance.

Retrieving her phone now would require moving, and she wasn't sure she could manage it. Not yet. God, please, not yet.

Then Michael's phone rang. Unlike hers, which he'd switched to vibrate, his device gave a short tweet that cut straight through their heavy breathing. She was tempted to hook her ankles behind his back and squeeze her tight inner muscles to make it impossible for him to leave, but she didn't.

Their magical time was over.

They'd set the trap. Now they would to see if the Bandit had taken the bait.

NEVER IN HIS life had Michael not wanted to answer a call. For fifteen minutes, he'd ignored his duty, his responsibilities, his good sense. Fifteen amazing, mind-blowing, life-changing minutes. And with each repetition of his phone's utilitarian trill, they drifted further from his grasp.

He wanted them back—but couldn't have them. Not now and perhaps not ever. He had to focus on his job. On catching the Bandit. On keeping Claire safe, not just for a quarter of an hour, but for the rest of her life.

With a short kiss and a groan, Michael slid out of the heaven that was Claire's body and retrieved his phone.

"He's on the move," Ruby said.

"You're sure it's him?"

"I'm sure it's the guy who was watching Claire's bedroom window with night vision binoculars, yeah. But for all we know, he's just a Peeping Tom and not the Bandit."

Night vision goggles? Why hadn't he thought about that?

He pushed his regrets aside and zeroed in on the operation. "Who's tailing him?"

"Me, but he's staying on foot."

Ruby was in a car. It would be hard for her to keep an eye on him without being noticed. Claire's street was only a few blocks from the heart of the French Quarter, but it might as well have been in a different world. It was quiet at this time of night. Nearly abandoned.

"And the rest of the team?"

"I ordered them to stay in their positions and watch the area around the house for any other activity. The tech is triangulating the call that came in to Claire's phone."

At this, Michael turned. Claire was sitting on the edge of the bed, naked in a way that she hadn't been before. Her body looked exposed, and her expression was wide-eyed and full of fear as she replayed the message from her cell phone.

He concentrated on talking to Ruby. "Any luck so far?"

"The call bounced off the same tower we're using," Ruby replied. "I think we've got him."

"Keep me updated."

He hung up just as Claire shut her own device down and started hunting in the dark for her clothes.

"What did his message say?"

She didn't answer, but set about untangling her panties so she could shove her legs into them. She snatched her jeans and performed the same maneuver, then patted the floor in search of her T-shirt and bra.

"Says he saw me. Saw us."

"We knew he would."

"He said he knew I'd be hot in bed." Her voice, so devoid of emotion, spoke volumes to her disgust. "He said he'd wanted to see me in action for a long time and thanked me for the show."

Michael forced himself to bite back a curse. Now wasn't the time for him to focus on his own rage. He had to concentrate on the unsub's motives.

His call was a taunt, an explosion of words meant to unnerve her, and the bomb had hit its target. She gave up on her bra and scrambled into her shirt before grabbing a pair of dark running shoes from the closet and then, to his dismay, her locked gun box.

"What do you think you're doing?" he asked.

She had the combination open in a split second, checked the ammunition of her Smith & Wesson and shoved it into the back of her jeans.

"What do you think I'm doing? Ruby's got eyes on the guy from across the street, right? Well, we can't do a damned thing with him until we're sure he's not just some sick Peeping Tom. We need proof he's the Bandit, or at least, enough evidence to warrant you going in officially. I'm going to get you that evidence."

He crossed his arms in front of him and blocked the door. "You can't go into his place, either. It's called breaking and entering."

She went up on her tiptoes to swipe a kiss across his cheek. "Only if I get caught."

When she attempted to slip around him, he grabbed her arm. She tried to yank free, but he held her fast. Just having a man they suspected to be the Bandit close enough to peer into her window and watch them make love was bad enough. He wasn't about to let her walk into the perv's lair, even if he was blocks away by now and couldn't return in a hurry without the agents noticing. Still, he'd gone to great lengths to keep Claire safe and he wasn't about to let her do something so reckless now.

Making love to her had transcended the sharing of sexual pleasure. The act of physically covering her body with his had reassured him that no other man would get his hands on her—no other man would touch her, taste her, learn the nuances and intricacies of her erogenous zones or hear the pleasured coos issuing from her well-kissed mouth.

Now she wanted to leave the apartment without him and break into a suspect's apartment with no backup?

"Claire, I can't let you—"

"You don't have a choice."

She tugged harder, shifting her body to a more advantageous stance.

He blocked her and glanced down at his vice-like grip. "I beg to differ."

She cursed, but gave up her physical struggle.

"How long do you plan to hold me here, Michael? How long until you either have to go join your team or the unsub gets back to his place, maybe to wash off Josslyn's blood? We've got a window of opportunity here and I'm not about to let it pass. You can't break any laws, I get that. But I'm an independent contractor. If I want to put my license on the line to find out if your people are following the right guy, it's my choice and you can't stop me."

His grip tightened, but his voice was low, measured—almost strangled.

"Watch me."

Michael could feel her determination just as he imagined she could smell his fear. How could he let her out of his sight now that they'd baited the Bandit so effectively? At the same time, she was right about her advantage in getting something solid on the man. His own team was bound by protocol, laws and procedures.

Claire only had the laws to worry about—and clearly, they didn't cause her much concern.

She locked her gaze with his. He could practically see her mind working as she tried to decide whether to scream, rage, or even tussle against his hold, but in the end, she merely took a deep breath and pushed out her words with calm authority.

"I can't live like this, Michael. I can't let some name-less, faceless unsub force me into hiding and I can't play by the rules. Those rules cost me my job with the force, but do you know why?"

He didn't respond. He'd read the official record and the newspaper clippings outlining how a rogue cop had gone against orders to investigate a death during Katrina that had been attributed to the storm, but had actually been a case of domestic violence. While Claire had never publically spoken out about the case, the parents of the victim had. They'd called her a hero. They'd lauded her dedication to the truth, even if it meant disobeying her superiors and losing her job.

"Because you care more about justice than you do about procedure?"

Her mouth dropped open a little in surprise, but she recovered quickly. "That about sums it up. We're cut from different fabrics, Michael. You're FBI—and thank God you are, because you're fighting the big fight, pro-tecting women like me from being victims of some sicko whose mommy didn't love him enough or who was born without a sanity gene. But your way can't always save the world. Sometimes, people like me, the ones who don't drink the Kool-Aid, can do some good, too."

She winced when he tightened his grip on her arms.

"I haven't had any spiked fruit punch, Claire. I believe in what I do."

"I know," she said, squirming until he loosened his hold. "And I swear to God, Michael, I respect you for it. But, at this moment, your way isn't getting the job done. Maybe the guy across the street was watching me. Maybe he called. But maybe he's not the Bandit. And we don't know if he has Josslyn. You need proof before you can execute a warrant—or compelling evidence that will convince a judge to let you in. If you let me go, I'll get that and you won't have to sully your hands or risk your career."

"My career isn't as important as your safety," he confessed.

"My safety doesn't mean anything if he hurts someone else instead. If he gives up on me, you'll have lost your only chance to stop him. I'm not going into this blind, Michael. I'm actually good at what I do."

He released her. She ran her hands up his chest, still bare, and pressed her cheek against his heart.

"From the moment you spirited me away from *Nouvelle Placage,* I've trusted you to do your job. Now, trust me to do mine."

He curved his body over hers and watched his father's ring catch a glimmer of light from a passing car. Under the influence of his family's legacy, he'd broken more rules than he could count, most in the last twenty-four hours. Could he really keep her from doing the same, particularly when what she might discover could help their case?

He released her. "You have ten minutes. Don't touch anything or move anything. If you see something that can help us, come back and let me know. If you contaminate any evidence, he'll get off. But you know all about that, don't you?"

Claire's entire face lit up in a smile. She gave him a saucy wink, and then snatched a bag she kept beside her bedroom door—one he suspected contained the tricks of her trade. A camera. Latex gloves. Booties for her shoes. More ammo.

"Thanks for trusting me, G-man. I won't let you down."

15

"WHAT DO YOU mean you lost him?"

Claire buried her face in her hands, the snap of latex chafing her skin. She ripped off her gloves and tossed them across the entryway. Michael slammed his hand against her banister, and even though she was sitting right below him on the bottom step, she barely flinched. If she wasn't so numb with fury, she might have kicked right through the drywall.

She'd done exactly what the FBI had needed her to do and they'd dropped the ball. The man who'd been across the street watching her make love to Michael with the night vision goggles she'd found dangling on a peg beside his windowsill had escaped.

Breaking into his apartment had been ridiculously easy—her first clue that he wanted to be discovered. Inside, she'd found a spy-shop worth of surveillance equipment, a refrigerator full of red roses and a hand-written diary that catalogued her every move over the last month. Since Michael had only allotted her a mere ten minutes to verify that the man who'd been watching them was indeed the Bandit, she'd used her remaining time to reset the clock feature on the guy's video camera, backing it up fifteen minutes or so, then she pointed the lens directly into her window and left.

Another tactic Michael would never have authorized, but she'd already tampered with the equipment, so he could do nothing but use it to his advantage.

The FBI needed probable cause to execute a search warrant. She'd given it to them by running home and ordering Michael to stay downstairs while she finished the last act in her operation of lies. After ditching her gear, she'd stripped down in the hallway, flashed on her bedroom light and run to the window, where she made a show of noticing the camera.

The whole set up had lasted all of fifteen minutes. By backing up the time feature, she'd synchronized the unsub's last phone call with his watching her in her bedroom—and provided Michael with the impetus he needed to get a warrant.

But while his superiors had worked on getting a judge to sign off on their search, Ruby's team had lost sight of the Bandit in a crowd on Bourbon Street.

"Did you at least get a good look at him? Enough to put together a sketch? A picture with your cell phone? What the hell, Ruby? We can't lose him now."

Rage radiated from Michael like fire banked in the belly of a dragon. Ruby was probably just as pissed off at herself as he was, but apologies could wait for another day.

Josslyn was in more danger than ever. Even if the FBI went through every inch of the lunatic's apartment, Claire was certain they wouldn't find anything to lead them to her.

So he'd left some equipment behind. If he'd recorded her, Claire hadn't found the files. A cursory look around, which was all Michael had given her time for, had not resulted in the discovery of a laptop or any other computer. The Bandit had abandoned what he no longer had use for.

He was leaving—which meant Josslyn's time was running out.

"Ruby, hold on. I've got a call. It's unknown. Could be our unsub."

At this, Claire jumped to her feet. She motioned for Michael to engage the speaker-phone feature, and to her surprise, he complied.

"Murrieta," he answered.

"You know, you really should have Alex show you how to say that correctly. You need to roll your r's."

Michael growled. "Damn it, Danny. I'm in the middle of a case. I thought I had my agents put you on a plane to California."

"In their defense, they did indeed provide me with a comfortable ride to the airport and even escorted me to the gate. But what they failed to do was walk me through security and forcibly buckle me into my seat."

"I'll make sure to be more specific next time," he grumbled.

"You do that," Danny said. "But I suggest you try it on someone else."

In the background, Claire heard the familiar thump and beat of a bass guitar—not the kind that came out of a stereo or juke box, but live music. Club music. Jazz club music endemic to the Quarter.

"Where are you?" she asked.

"Claire, my darling. I'd hoped I could count on you to cut to the crux of the matter. I'm at a righteous bar on the far end of Bourbon Street. The music is phenomenal and the women are getting drunker by the minute, and yet, am I taking advantage? Spending my last night in the Big Easy drunk on wine, women and song? No, I'm calling my brother."

"And why the hell would you do that?" Michael asked.

"I'm wounded," Danny said, his laissez faire attitude crawling underneath her skin. "Can't I just have missed you?"

"No," Claire and Michael barked in unison.

Danny chuckled. "You're right. I don't miss either one of you. In fact, I don't miss much at all. That's probably a big part of the reason why I'm so damned great at my job."

"Stealing things?" Michael snapped.

"Usually, though in this case, finding things. You see, first I found you tonight at Claire's. Nice little show in the window, though from the rooftop across the street, I couldn't see much once you killed the lights."

Michael went to disengage the speaker phone feature, but Claire stayed his hand. She didn't give a damn if Michael's brother had seen her completely naked and in the throes of a glorious orgasm—he'd called for a reason.

"Too bad for you," she shot back. "Your brother's quite the stud. You might have learned something. So you found us. Is that it?"

"Not by a longshot, darlin'. First I found you. Then I spotted Ruby trying to follow someone down the street in a car when he was on foot. I mean, honestly? Is that any way to operate? So I decided to help her out. Help *you* out. I hope you remember this." Danny had to raise his voice to overcome the applause that had just erupted behind him.

Claire met Michael's incensed gaze. Danny was stringing them along for his own amusement, but they both read between the lines. He'd followed the same guy

Ruby had followed—their suspect. But unlike the FBI agent, who'd been trapped in her car, he'd been on foot.

Danny wasn't calling just to give his brother and Claire a hard time. That was just the icing. The cake was that he'd found their unsub—and knew precisely where he was.

MICHAEL LEFT ONE agent at the unsub's apartment and had the other three, including Ruby, meet him at the Bourbon Street bar. Danny waited for them inside, sipping a draft beer while he kept an eye on the staircase that led to the upper floors. He'd done a quick sweep around back, and while he'd discovered an old, rickety fire escape leading down from the third floor, the seasoned criminal had quickly determined that no one had used it in half a century.

And lived.

Still, the first thing Michael did was post a local cop to watch it from below.

The second thing he did was try to send Claire home.

He really didn't know why he'd bothered. She'd refused police protection, and since she knew the property owner of the bar where Danny was staked out, Michael decided she was more useful with him than fighting him. She'd already texted the building's owner and learned that the current tenant of the third-floor loft had been some kind of recording artist who'd put a layer of sound-proofing on the floors at his own expense and had spent quite a bit of time shopping for antiques on Royal Street.

If the tenant was the Bandit, he'd created a perfect lair for his fantasy seduction.

Nice guy the man had texted. Quiet until lately. Pays cash.

Until lately? Claire had texted back.

The property owner replied quickly. Had a complaint from my cleaning staff this morning about what sounded like a woman screaming, but I went up and checked. Everything was in order.

A woman screaming? Josslyn, perhaps? Hidden where the landlord couldn't find her?

Michael checked his sidearm. "You stay here," he ordered Claire, before commanding Ruby to remain behind with her.

"I don't need a babysitter and you need Ruby to watch your back more than you need her to watch mine," she argued.

"I'm not leaving you out here in the open. For all we know, he's planned this. He's led us here just so he can get to you."

"Now you're being paranoid," she sniped.

"Maybe," he replied. "But I'm not taking any chances with your life."

"But you'll take chances with your own? That's noble. And stupid."

Ruby cleared her throat. "There is another option."

They both turned to her, Michael with a glare and Claire with a grin that cemented their friendship for life.

"And what the hell is that?"

Ruby shrugged apologetically, as if she knew that what she was about to suggest was not going to go over well. "Danny."

"Someone say my name?"

Startled by Danny's approach, Michael clutched at the cell phone in his hand, nearly cracking the casing.

"Jumpy nerves," Danny said, tsking disapprovingly. "Bad sign, bro."

"I thought you were our eyes inside?" he asked.

"With all these prettier eyes out here? Besides, I saw

one of your guys move in. He's practically sitting on the staircase. Your suspect isn't going anywhere."

"Good."

Michael watched his brother give Claire a sideways glance, one that was a little more appraising than he'd like. While there was a chance that the unsub was up-stairs in his soundproofed lair with Josslyn Granger, there was also a chance he was lurking somewhere nearby, waiting for Claire to be alone so he could grab her. Michael couldn't risk having her so vulnerable, even if that meant leaving her with his brother.

Her phone buzzed. She looked at the LCD screen, and even in the blinking neon lights outside the jazz club, he watched her face go white.

She flipped the phone so he could see. *Unknown Caller.*

He dug his hands into his pockets, retrieved his keys and shoved them into Danny's hands. "Get her out of here."

"What? No!" Claire objected. "I'm not in any danger down here. You, go do your thing, but don't make me leave."

Danny wrapped his arm protectively over Claire's shoulder for a split second before she shrugged him off. Michael didn't trust his brother as far as he could throw him, but he did trust Claire. And though Danny was a selfish son-of-a-bitch with delusions of grandeur, he had helped them out.

He pointed his finger in Danny's face. "If anything happens to her, I'll kill you."

Danny rolled his eyes. "Yeah, yeah. Macho point taken. Go get the bad guy. I'll take care of the damsel in distress."

Michael waited until Claire launched into a full-blown

attack on Danny's misconceptions about the state of her distress before he motioned for his team to follow him to a quieter location so they could formulate a plan of attack. He suddenly wasn't worried for Claire, but his brother was another story entirely.

"OKAY, OKAY. I surrender!" Danny said, holding up both of his hands. "My jaw still aches from the last time you proved you didn't need anyone to protect you. Just consider me an extra set of eyes, okay. I'm yours to command."

Claire walked to the other side of the car, her gaze locked on Danny, who might have thought he was looking all magnanimous, when he really just looked like a jerk. She was starting to understand why Michael wasn't his half-brother's biggest fan. Daniel Burnett was tall, dark, handsome and charming—but he was also smug, condescending and full of himself.

"You love pissing people off, don't you?" she asked.

He grinned and leaned on the hood of the car. "I do, I really do. My profession normally doesn't allow for much human interaction. So when I'm in the company of men—or women—I like to make the experience memorable."

"Even if it's in a bad way?"

"I take what I can get," he said proudly.

"Literally and figuratively."

He gave her a small half-bow. "Touché."

Danny held out his hand to her, and with a smirk, she decided to join him. His side of the car had a better vantage point. She chafed at watching Michael from a distance, waiting on the sidelines while he and his team planned their next move without her input.

She ached to be a part of whatever was going down,

but as much as it killed her to remain behind, she had to let the professionals do their jobs. She tried to alleviate some of her pent up adrenaline by bouncing on her toes, but the action only annoyed Danny. He placed a firm hand on her shoulder.

"You need a drink," he assessed.

"I need to see Josslyn Granger walk out of that building safe and sound."

"You really think there's a chance of that?"

"Yes," she answered quickly…maybe a little too quickly. The fact that the Bandit had tried to contact her again, but this time had not left a message, was prickling at the back of her neck.

"Are you sure the suspect couldn't have gotten out of the building without you seeing him?"

Danny shrugged. "Not unless he has some secret exit no one knows about."

Claire yanked her phone out of her back pocket and started texting the building owner just as Michael and his team headed into the building. She tapped her fingers nervously on the screen of her phone while she waited for a reply.

Then it came.

Used to be a staircase that came out next to the bakery on Dumaine. Stairs crumbled years ago. Sealed it for building code.

Unfortunately, seals could be broken.

Michael and his team were out of sight, going into the building when there was suddenly a chance that the Bandit wasn't inside.

Claire started across the street.

"Where are you going?" Danny asked, close at her heels.

"Checking out a lead."

"Not a good idea." He made a swipe for her arm, but she dodged him.

"Says you," she replied, lowering her voice as they approached the back alley. The corner property was an old bakery which had closed over a decade ago. Longer and wider than the club, the building created alleys and a courtyard not easily visible from the street.

She accessed the flashlight app on her cell phone, then slid through a dark passage, turning and twisting around garbage cans and abandoned crates until she found the narrow break between the two buildings. She searched for marks in the wall that might have once covered a door, but the brick had been repaired in so many places, it was hard to see any suspicious grooves.

Instead, she looked down, hissing at Danny to stay where he was at the edge of the passageway while she searched the ground.

"Here," she said, kneeling down beside a man-size boot print that seemed to have appeared from nowhere.

"What?"

She handed him the phone while she used her hands to feel around the wall. Just as she felt a break in the brick, her cell phone buzzed.

She snatched the device before Danny had a chance to intervene.

Unknown Caller.

Only, he wasn't unknown, was he? It was the Bandit. And this time, she answered his call.

16

"THIS IS CLAIRE."

Her voice quavered, so she took a deep breath and tried to steady the flow of adrenaline shooting through her body. From the thick walls of the jazz club, the heartbeat of New Orleans pumped out above the thrum of the music and muffled laughter of the crowd. Somewhere just on the other side, Michael was making his way through the swell of inebriated, sweaty, swaying people, on his way to catch a dangerous criminal who wasn't even there.

"I know where you are," the man said, his voice deep, his accent distinctively Hispanic. Real or fake? Claire couldn't tell. Not unless she got him to talk more.

She held her other hand flat against Danny's chest, keeping him still. He'd flipped out his cell phone, but she shook her head violently. He couldn't call Michael now. Any distraction might mean disaster. Donny grimaced, but started typing anyway.

"Are you watching me?" she asked, her eyes scanning the area. Tucked deep in the hidden alley, she couldn't imagine anyone could see her clearly. But he might have watched her go into the dark and knew that unless she discovered a way into his secret passage, she'd have no other escape route.

"I haven't stopped watching you for weeks, *preciosa*. Why would I stop now?"

"Because I'm on to you. I'm going to catch you."

She kept her pronouns singular, but they sounded foreign on her tongue. She wasn't just *I* anymore. She was *we*. She and Michael. Did he realize it as well? Did he accept it?

Could she?

The Bandit's elaborate scheme to lure them to this building forced her to accept that he knew they were on to him. Whether or not he realized his hunter was both an FBI agent and a true Murrieta descendent who didn't take too kindly to having his family legacy soiled by this man's sick sexual games, she couldn't be sure.

"What do you want?"

"What I've always wanted. You. And you alone."

"What if I said you can't have me?"

He laughed. "I'd say you were playing hard to get, a game I'd usually appreciate, only now I've run out of time. No more time for play. And I'm afraid I can't come sweep you up myself. You'll have to come to me."

"I can't do that," she replied. She couldn't make this easy—he'd expect her to put up a fight. Paulette had resisted Joaquin for months, according to the diary. But with Josslyn's life on the line, Claire couldn't toy with him for long.

"You must, unless you want that woman's misery on your head."

From the other side of the building, she heard the clomping sound of hooves on the pavement. It wasn't unusual for carriages to circle through the French Quarter in the evenings, shuttling tourists from place to place, but not at this time of night. Most drivers stabled their mules by ten o'clock so they didn't have to deal with the drunks.

Drivers were available for special hire, though.

Danny opened his mouth to speak, but she put her finger to her lips.

"Where do you want me to go?"

"I've arranged your transportation," he said. "But before you embark on your journey, you need to get rid of your...gentleman friend."

Claire's gaze shot up. He had to be watching her, but from where? The only windows in the alley were on the third floor. At this very moment, Michael was likely up there busting into the Bandit's studio apartment. So where was the guy?

"Fine," she said, waving her hand to encourage Danny to pull one of his infamous disappearing acts.

Instead, he crossed his arms over his chest. She rolled her eyes. Apparently, the Murrieta overprotective gene was alive and well in Daniel Burnett. She continued to gesture, hoping he could somehow understand he should back off, but not go far. Then she realized that the Bandit would think it was weird if she didn't actually speak out loud to her companion.

"Hey, Michael," she said, using his brother's name so he'd clue in that her request was not entirely genuine. "I don't see any doorway here. Why don't you go around and check the other side?"

Danny arched an eyebrow, but he stepped closer so the Bandit could hear his end of the conversation. "I can't leave you alone."

"Where am I going to go?" she asked with an uncomfortable laugh. "It's a dead end. I'm safe. Go on. We have to find Josslyn."

"Okay, but I'm going to come right back for you. Don't move."

Danny winked.

"I won't."

He leaned into her opposite ear and whispered, "I'll be right behind you."

Claire nodded, swallowing when Danny swept his hand across her cheek in an intimate gesture that reminded her forcefully of his brother. Michael would hit the roof if he realized Danny was leaving her alone, even if only for the span of a heartbeat. But what choice did they have? If she didn't at least pretend to be cooperating, Josslyn could pay with her life.

Claire realized that while the Bandit might not be upstairs with Josslyn anymore, he had her. Somewhere. Claire had gotten the woman into this mess—she owed it to her to get her out.

Danny moved toward the alley exit, his thumbs flying across the screen of his phone as he disappeared around the corner. She was sure he was texting Michael, who likely wouldn't see the message until his bust of the upstairs studio was over and he discovered that the man they'd been looking for wasn't there.

When Danny left, the air in the alley left with him. She was alone. Vulnerable. Just what the Bandit had wanted all along—just what Michael had put his career on the line to avoid since he'd first popped into her life at *Nouvelle Placage*.

It seemed like a lifetime ago. Her only real concern then had been tracking down a woman with a sex fetish. That night, in her sensual costume with the strains of romantic music floating on the air along with the scents of flowers and candle wax, Claire's concern about the man who'd sent her the monogrammed scarf had been at the back of her mind. She'd planned to deal with that problem once she closed her case, banked the second half of her fee and ensured that two little children had a mother who loved them.

The Bandit had managed to make her vulnerable, but she wasn't entirely unprepared. She still had her gun. And she wasn't alone. Somewhere not too far away, Danny was lurking, attempting to contact his brother.

"Okay, he's gone."

A trill from behind her nearly made her jump out of her skin. A cell phone? A blue light glowed from underneath a scattering of discarded beer bottles.

"Answer it," the Bandit said.

"What?"

"Answer the phone I left for you. Now."

She complied, not surprised to hear his voice on the other end. "Now turn off your other phone. Can't have anyone using it to track you down."

Claire cursed silently.

"Fine." She disconnected the call, but put her phone— still powered up—in her back pocket.

"Toss it."

"Sure," she agreed. She snatched one of the empty beer bottles and hefted it to the other side of the alley.

"If you still have the phone on you when you arrive," he warned, his singsong voice powerfully menacing, "I will be very angry."

She continued to peer into the darkness. He had to be watching her from somewhere, but he wasn't close enough to see that she'd made a switch. A parade of curses marched through her head, but she pressed her lips together tightly, reining in her frustration.

She had to keep cool. He was already playing her by threatening to hurt Josslyn. She couldn't allow him to manipulate her into making any bigger mistakes than she was already in by staying here and talking to him.

"The phone is gone," she lied.

"Good," the Bandit replied. "Now walk back to Dumaine. There, my lady, your carriage awaits."

She retraced her steps and emerged from the alley. Her gaze darted up and around, but buildings in this area were closely packed and many storied. The Bandit could be watching her from anywhere—or from nowhere at all. Security cameras were dotted throughout the Quarter. Had he somehow tapped into the feed? And, if so, what would he do when he realized Danny was on her tail?

If Danny managed to keep up with the mule and buggy waiting for her at the sidewalk.

"You Paulette?" the driver asked.

"Say yes," the Bandit said into her ear.

She nodded. It was a tiny defiance the Bandit let slide. The driver, an old and tired man she might have seen once or twice in the Quarter, gave a cursory nod and waved her up.

"What's our destination?" she asked.

"That's a surprise," the driver said, practically in unison with the criminal on the other end of the phone.

The man snapped the reins and the carriage jerked forward. Claire figured that she wasn't the only person in for a big surprise—Michael was going to get a hell of a shock when he realized she was gone.

"Is she alive?"

Michael holstered his weapon the minute one of his team members yelled, "Clear!" He dropped to the ground beside Ruby, who was checking Josslyn Granger's crumpled body for a pulse.

"She's got a heartbeat," she announced, then bent her face closer to Josslyn's. The woman's skin was pale, her makeup smeared off, leaving very little to remind him of the boldly sensual woman he'd met only the night before. "She's breathing, but she's out cold. Probably drugged."

Ruby shouted for the other agents to look around for a syringe or pill bottle while she moved the woman into a more comfortable position. Michael whipped out his phone to dial for an ambulance when he noticed the flashing icon that signaled he had a text message from Daniel.

His heart seized in his chest. Daniel was supposed to be watching Claire. And the Bandit, who had skillfully lured them to this third floor studio, was nowhere to be found.

"Call 9-1-1," he ordered Ruby, and then retrieved his text messages.

He read the thread of Danny's messages, his soul leeching out with each word.

2:18 a.m.: Bandit on phone with Claire. Not in club!
2:19 a.m.: Claire found hidden exit from 3rd floor to back alley. Bandit gone.
2:22 a.m.: Bandit trading Claire for Josslyn. I'm following. Call me.

He couldn't breathe—not without burning his lungs from the inside out. He blinked away a sudden wave of nauseating dizziness and stumbled toward the door, his fingers fumbling with the Call Back feature.

"Michael, what's wrong?" Ruby shouted.

He pushed the words out of his mouth, nearly doubling

over with the pain of saying them out loud. "The Bandit has Claire."

Vaguely aware of footsteps following behind him as he clattered down the metal stairs, he stumbled out into the street just as Danny picked up his call.

"Where are you?" he demanded.

His brother sounded winded and spoke in a hushed voice Michael could barely hear over the revelry pouring out of the club. He shot across to the car, cursing when he realized he had no keys.

Danny had the keys.

Danny, who was barely audible now. "...down on Burgundy. Three mules and buggies. All with one woman inside. Wait, I think I have her."

He gave his general location just before the call cut out.

"Danny? Danny?"

He hadn't had enough time to curse when Ruby slid into the driver's side and ducked under the dashboard. Five interminable seconds later, the car sprang to life.

"Where to?" she asked.

Michael jumped into the passenger seat, told Ruby where Danny had last been and then tried to return Danny's call. He went straight into voicemail, so he switched tactics and texted Claire that Josslyn was safe and that she should not do anything the Bandit told her to do.

He said the words aloud as he typed, hoping without hope that Claire was still in a position to read his plea.

17

CLAIRE FELT THE buzz in her pocket, but she didn't dare retrieve her phone. The driver seemed wholly uninterested in her, not even bothering with the make-believe New Orleans history lessons a lot of buggy drivers engaged in with tourists.

But that didn't mean she wasn't being watched.

She knew the neighborhood fairly well. This stretch of Ursulines Avenue was quiet in the dead of night, but not abandoned. If she screamed now, someone might hear her—if they didn't just assume she was a Bourbon Street partier who had lost her way.

The homes here were old and built for sturdiness. If the Bandit had managed to soundproof the studio apartment at the top of a popular jazz club, there was no telling what he'd do with an entire building.

Not surprisingly, the driver pulled up in front of a house on the corner.

"This is it," he said.

"Say nothing," the Bandit instructed. He'd remained on the phone the entire ride over, though Claire had tried to tune him out. While he'd spent the time rhapsodizing over her beauty and describing a sampling of the pleasures that awaited her at his hideaway, she'd been trying to figure out where she was going and what the hell she was going to do once she got there.

Now she was here. It was time to act.

She got out of the carriage, gave the driver a friendly wave and watched him snap his reins and continue down the street. She gave the neighborhood a quick once over. The abundance of low hanging tree branches did not erase the fact that most of the front yards had brick or stone walls in front of them, making it hard for anyone to walk down the sidewalk without being spotted—even an international art thief. Still, she had to trust that Danny wasn't going to let her down.

"Come in," the Bandit said. "The gate is open."

While she pretended to futz with the lock on the gate, she reached into her back pocket and dropped her original phone onto a patch of soft ground by the fence. She waited for the Bandit to comment on her action, but when he didn't, she figured she was in the clear.

If Michael was still tracking her cell phone, he'd be able to find her. She just had to hold the Bandit off for a little while, maybe make sure she'd located Josslyn before the cavalry arrived. When she turned to close and latch the gate, she glanced down at her phone and saw the latest text message on the screen.

We have Josslyn.

Her hand slipped. If Michael had Josslyn, she had no reason to be here. She fumbled with the metal latch when a gloved hand snaked around her neck and pressed on her throat.

"Now I have you."

THE ONLY THING that stopped Michael from shooting his brother on the spot was the fact that the minute Ruby screeched to a stop outside the seemingly dark and un-inhabited house on Ursulines Avenue, Danny leaped down from a dark section of the eight-foot-tall fence and landed beside him with barely a sound.

"They're on the second floor, east side of the house. A bedroom, naturally."

"Why didn't you break in and help her?"

"I'm a lover, not a fighter," Danny shot back. "I'm also not entirely stupid. The guy is armed and I knew you were minutes away. He took her gun before he even let her over the threshold. Tossed it in the fountain. By the time I retrieved it, it was useless."

"Get us in," he said to Danny, who then clamped him on the shoulder and motioned for them to follow him into the darkness.

How he'd found the man-size break in the stone wall, masked by a thick bush that smelled like hibiscus on one side and bougainvillea on the other, Michael would never know. But as Danny had managed to successfully tail the Bandit twice now, he realized he'd be a fool not to trust the man's instincts.

As he attempted to keep his movements minimal and silent, Michael watched Danny move across the lawn like a shadow created by branches and moonlight. Soundlessly, he launched himself onto a porch railing and flipped up onto the roof that ran around the entire length of the house.

He dropped to his belly and extended both hands.

Michael motioned for Ruby to go. He preferred a more direct route.

"Alarm?"

Danny, still lying prone with Ruby beside him,

grinned. "I took the liberty of disengaging it before you showed up. Hope you don't mind. I know you hate for me to be a part of your investigation."

Michael couldn't decide whether to respond wryly to the crack or thank him profusely, so he opted to say nothing at all.

Once inside the house, he took a moment to establish his bearings, then headed up the stairs in the direction Danny had indicated. The house was large and devoid of furniture, so his every step echoed. Once he reached the upstairs corridor to the bedrooms, he found two doors that could lead to Claire. He leaned his ear against both, but neither revealed any sound. He couldn't make a mistake.

He flattened his palm on the closest door. His father's ring sparkled dully in the dim light. He slid across to the other one. This time, the emerald seemed to flash a little brighter.

He stepped back, leveled a flat-footed kick just below the door knob and watched the frame splinter as pain shot up his leg and a scream rent the air. Weapon drawn, he charged into the room at nearly the same time that Ruby tumbled in through a shattered window.

It took a second before Michael registered that neither Claire nor Ruby had been the one to scream.

Claire stood menacingly over a man, dressed entirely in black satin, who was rolling around on the ground clutching at his crotch. "I warned you not to touch me, didn't I?"

"Man, I hope this guy bought home owner's insurance," Danny quipped, artfully tumbling through the cracked glass. He surveyed the scene, then winced. "And an athletic supporter."

Claire leaned forward, hands on knees. "The bastard tried to drug me."

Danny sauntered over, picked up a wine bottle now spilling its contents over the faded rug and took a whiff. "Bad year."

"Things are about to get worse," Michael said, pulling out his handcuffs.

He and Ruby secured the Bandit, but left him on the floor. They called for backup, then gestured Claire over so she could snatch the black mask off his face.

She frowned. "Never seen him."

The man had regained his ability to speak, though his voice spiked high at first before settling into a raspy accent. "Of course you saw me! I was everywhere you were. Everywhere. Couldn't you feel my eyes on you? My passion heating up your body—"

Claire shoved the mask in his mouth and marched out of the room.

Michael finished up his call to the agents still processing the jazz club crime scene, but before he could speak to Claire, who was standing on the top landing overlooking the desolate interior of the rental home with Danny, the police arrived.

This, of course, caused Danny to disappear. Claire remained alone, silently watching as the local cops processed the scene. Then, with Ruby at her side, she completed an extensive interview with a pair of detectives, one of whom Claire seemed to know.

Twenty minutes passed before Michael found her again, and they were twenty minutes too long. The entire time he'd liaised with the police, engaged in a brief preliminary interrogation of the suspect—who still refused to give his name—and supervised the processing of the crime scene to ensure that enough evidence was gathered to put this creep in federal prison for a long time, he'd wanted to be with Claire.

His muscles ached with the absence of her. His senses seemed to reach out from wherever he was to catch a sight or scent of her. Even a murmured echo of her voice from the hallway had sent the blood thrumming through his body as if attempting to propel him near her, to comfort her, to help her through the terror she must have felt when the Bandit had captured her.

Claire had said she could take care of herself. Clearly, she hadn't been exaggerating.

"I'll take over," Ruby said, coming up beside Michael at the back of the room where he stood watching the crime scene photographers.

"Yeah?" he asked.

She grinned. "I've never seen you so antsy. She's fine, but she needs you. Go."

Claire sat on the top step. She leaned her head against the banister, clearly exhausted. He snatched a blanket from the paramedics and wrapped it around her shoulders as he sat beside her. The front of her T-shirt was stained with red, probably the wine the Bandit had dosed with Rohypnol. The wet fabric instantly reminded him that she wasn't wearing a bra.

Not something he should be thinking about, but he couldn't help himself. His desire for Claire went beyond the physical—but the physical was still pretty powerful stuff.

She shifted to lean against him.

"So," she said, her voice bone weary. "How angry are you?"

"Why would I be angry?" he asked, turning so that her cheek slipped off his shoulder to press against his chest.

"Um, because I left Danny behind and walked right into the very same dangerous situation you've been working so hard to keep me out of?"

He chuckled and held her closer. From the side, he noticed a couple of his colleagues staring, but he didn't care. Soon enough, everyone was going to know that he'd been involved with the subject of his investigation. Maybe it was the ring's influence, but he didn't care.

"Yeah, well, there is that. But you took care of yourself, just like you promised you would. I promised to protect you. That part didn't work out so well."

She sat back, glowering at him. "What are you talking about? You did protect me. It took a lot of guts to leave me in your brother's hands, and I have to say, for a guy who's spent the majority of his life breaking the law, he did a great job of keeping track of me and making sure you got to me as fast as possible. And it was your text message that changed everything. If you hadn't let me know that Josslyn was safe, I wouldn't have fought back so hard. Once I knew she was alive, I had nothing to lose."

"But I had everything to lose. For one horrible moment I don't ever want to relive, I thought I'd lost you."

Her mouth curved downward, but her eyes seemed alight with energy. "You really think I'm that easy to get rid of?"

"God, I hope not."

Michael wrapped his arms around her, tugging her close and breathing in the scent of her shampooed hair, the hygienic blanket and the drug-infused wine. Around him, he was vaguely aware of people moving, talking, maybe even asking questions, but he remained in the warm cocoon of their bodies.

He could not let her go. Physically, he'd manage it, but beyond that? There was no way. Over the course of two short days, they'd connected in ways he'd never experienced with any other woman—and this was a treasure more priceless than his father's ring or his ancestor's romantic legacy. Using a sword or whip, wearing a mask and riding through the night to right wrongs was nothing compared with the courage Michael now needed to surrender his heart.

Only, he'd already surrendered it, hadn't he? That first night in the bedroom, when he'd tossed aside the protocols of his job for a chance to kiss the woman of his dreams.

A cadre of local FBI agents marched down the stairs, turning in unison to stare disapprovingly in his direction. At their frowns, Claire sighed and broke the magical bubble that had encased them.

"You're going to be in a lot of trouble, aren't you? For fraternizing or something?"

"Or something," he said, chuckling at the idea. It was ridiculous. Absurd. A week ago, he would have cared if his superiors had questioned his professionalism. Now, not so much.

"Anything I can do?"

"Yeah, actually," he said, rising to his feet and taking her hands to pull her up with him. "How do you feel about taking on a partner? For your P.I. business, I mean."

It was a good thing he hadn't released her because her foot stumbled down a step and she nearly took a tumble.

"What?"

"Look, the only reason I wasn't with you tonight, to really protect you, was because I had to put my job first. I had to go after Josslyn and I have no regrets I did that, but being away from you, being constrained by the rules and regulations of my job…it's starting to chafe. Remember when I gave you ten minutes to sneak over to the unsub's apartment and look around and you found the evidence we needed? Part of me was terrified that he'd come back and hurt you, but the other part of me was jealous as hell that you could break the rules in the first place."

She tossed the blanket off her shoulders and stepped onto the landing. Only now did Michael realize that the second floor of the house was entirely empty of people, though he could hear Ruby talking downstairs. She'd probably herded everyone out of the way to give him and Claire real privacy—a privacy he was going to take advantage of, no matter how much his revelations shocked her.

"I don't understand," she said. "You're quitting the Bureau?"

"Yeah," he said, surprised by how easy the answer came.

Her eyes widened. "And you're doing this just because you were jealous that I could break the law to get what we needed and you couldn't?"

"It's more than that. God, so much more."

Unable to stand another second without touching her, Michael took her hands again, this time indulging in his need to kiss her by pressing his lips first against her knuckles and then her wrists and palms.

"You don't know a lot about my life or my past," he confessed. "That's nothing unusual with the women in my life because I've never taken the time to give them a piece of me. I was too wrapped up in my career, in my ambitions, in my unending need to prove that I'm one of the good guys, no matter what ne'er-do-wells and bandits have peppered my past."

"Michael, I've met a lot of good guys and bad guys, and trust me, you're one of the best."

"Maybe," he said, heat rising in his cheeks in a way that might have embarrassed him with any other woman. But not with Claire. With her, he could feel anything, say anything, do anything. As if she'd had a key to unlock his soul. "But I don't want to be defined by my past anymore. I don't want to be defined by my job. I want to be defined by doing what I love, with someone I love."

She slipped her arms around his neck and kissed him. With her tongue, she parted the last of his resistance, and as she melted in his arms, his heart fused into her. They had so many things left to say to one another—so many things to learn and share. But he knew without a moment's hesitation that he wanted to explore all the possibilities life and love had to offer—with Claire and only Claire.

"I love you, too," Claire said, breaking away just enough to run her hands over his face and then spear them into his hair. "I've known you for two days and I love you, Michael Murrieta."

"It sounds crazy," he replied, but no crazier than what he felt.

She threw back her head and laughed. "My life has always been crazy, but I never imagined the insanity was just a prelude to this. If I had, I might have spent more time enjoying it."

"We'll enjoy it together from now on. How does that sound?"

Unable to resist any longer, he dipped his head and kissed the soft flesh on her neck. The way she cooed in his ear and clutched at his shoulders gave him a hint as to her answer.

"Sounds wild, Michael. Too wild."

He braced her spine with his hand so that she arched her back, giving him clearer access to her throat.

"There's no such thing as too wild, Claire. Not with us. Not ever."

Epilogue

THE GOLD RING clattered over the felt tabletop, but Daniel instantly caught it, not giving the family heirloom a chance to roll off the side or get mistaken for an up of his ante. The shock of holding the ring for the first time caught him unaware, and it took him a split second to realize that Michael had shooed away the dealer at the private blackjack table he'd been gambling at for the past hour.

"You were going to leave without saying goodbye?" Michael asked, sliding into the tall chair beside his.

Daniel grumbled, slid the ring onto the table in front of his brother, then shook the ice in the bottom of his tumbler to get one last taste of the Scotch. "I'm not big on goodbyes."

"You pretty much suck at hellos, too."

"I don't generally like to announce my presence to people coming or going," he explained. "Hurts my chances of ripping them off if they realize I'm around."

Michael caught the attention of a passing cocktail waitress, ordered two drinks and then turned back to his brother. He gave him a powerful once-over that made Daniel yearn for a dark corner or shadow in which to disappear. Unfortunately, those were tough to come by in a brilliantly lit casino.

Unlike Alejandro, whose assessing stare tended toward the judgmental and was, therefore, easy to brush off, Michael's gaze was more probing—as if he didn't quite know what to make of his middle brother. As if he were a puzzle he desperately wanted to solve.

Daniel knew the feeling. He'd been trying to figure himself out his whole life, but never more than in the last few months. His brothers had forced the issue. Not because they'd wanted to and certainly not because he'd asked them to redefine who he was.

It was all because of the ring.

Just two months ago, he'd started on a path to retrieve his father's most prized possession. He'd only met Ramon Murrieta once. He'd used the opportunity to let the old man know. He'd survived foster care without his intervention, so he sure as hell didn't need him once he'd turned eighteen. He'd built his own family with a menagerie of thieves, fences, money-launderers and loan sharks.

The irony had not escaped him that years later, when he'd been unfairly accused of attempted murder, that "family" had deserted him. If not for Lucienne, his adopted sister, and the two brothers he did not know, he would have been entirely alone

And now, the brother who'd been the most doubtful of Daniel's motives, the one who had grown up with Ramon Murrieta and deserved his legacy more than anyone, had tried to give him their father's ring?

Again, Michael slid the emerald in front of Daniel. This time, he didn't pick it up.

"What's this for?" he asked.

Michael grinned. "Don't need it anymore."

"I didn't realize the wearer had to need it," he said. "I thought it was just about blood."

"Didn't Alex tell you what the ring does?"

Daniel scoffed. "Said something about the three qualities of Joaquin Murrieta or some shit. I wasn't listening," he lied.

He'd heard every word Alex had told him, of course, but how could he believe in such nonsense? Over the course of his career, he'd stolen more than a few items purported to have curses or luck associated with them and he'd never seen anything to make him believe the legends were even remotely based in truth.

But Alex, a dyed-in-the-wool skeptic of epic proportions, had given the ring credit for bringing him together with Lucienne. And from the grin on Michael's face, he had also found the path to true love and was assigning some of the credit to the hunk of well-worn gold and damaged stones.

Daniel lifted his glass again, hoping for one last drop of Scotch. "Great. I'll sell it."

Michael's smile did not falter. "No, you won't."

He was right. Just a couple of months ago, someone had wanted the ring so badly, they'd set Daniel up to take a murder rap. If he put the ring back on to the open market, that still unknown person might get it—and Daniel's vengeful nature wouldn't allow that to happen.

To keep the ring safe, it would have to stay in the family.

"I don't need a woman in my life," he said, tossing the emerald across the table. Michael caught it on a bounce.

"Oh, the ring isn't about women. It's about giving you what you're missing."

Daniel waved him off, not wanting to hear a lecture

about which aspects of his character needed a magical intervention. "I'm not missing anything."

Michael used the opportunity to snatch his hand. "Trust me, bro, you need this."

Their wrestling caught the attention of the gamblers nearby, but before anyone could intervene, the burlier Michael had succeeded in sliding the ring onto Daniel's finger. He tried to tug it off, but couldn't get it past his knuckle.

Michael sat down on his chair and shook his clothes back into place.

"What the hell?" Daniel protested.

"Consider it a favor, brother. Your life has been going nowhere. Maybe you need a change. The ring might give it to you. Look at me. I've decided to take a break from the Bureau. I'm staying in New Orleans. With Claire."

Danny gave the ring one last tug, then gave up. He'd ice his hand later. Maybe use some soap. In the meantime, he could at least admire the craftsmanship. If not for the Z-shaped scratch on the emerald and the somewhat sloppy repairs made to the worn gold band, it might have fetched a nice price in a foreign market.

Maybe he would still try, just to get rid of the thing.

Or maybe he'd see what the piece of crap jewelry could do.

The cocktail waitress returned with two glasses of Bourbon, neat. They each took a sip. Daniel preferred Scotch but the alcoholic burn on his tongue was nice all the same.

"So you're sticking around to study for your P.I. license?"

"Wouldn't be too hard, with my experience. And I have a bead on an internship with a local P.I. who for some reason seems to want me around."

Michael put his glass down and leaned in close so his whispered words could be heard over the dinging bells and endless chatter on the casino's main floor.

"Thanks for keeping an eye on her. You kept your word. That means a lot."

Daniel eyed his brother intently. "For future reference, I'm a thief, not a liar."

"I didn't realize the two were mutually exclusive."

"Don't get me wrong. To be an effective thief, lying is often part of the deal. But I try to avoid it when I can."

"So you'll tell me the truth if I ask you whether or not you came to New Orleans just to steal Pop's ring?"

"If you asked," Danny said, hoping he wouldn't.

"Then I'm asking."

Daniel frowned and looked down at his hand. He hadn't really expected it to fit. He remembered his father's fingers being thicker and longer than his own. He'd met him only once, but he still remembered the strength in the old man's hands.

He threw back the remaining Bourbon, impressed by how the light caught on the green stone, despite the scratch.

"The thought had occurred to me, yes, but then I asked myself, where was the challenge? You were so distracted by Claire and the Bandit, you wouldn't have noticed if I'd cut your finger off to get it."

Michael arched a brow. "So the only reason you take things that don't belong to you is for the challenge?"

Daniel laughed. In the beginning, he'd stolen to survive. Once he'd figured out he was good at it, he'd done it for the sense of accomplishment—and the cash.

But since Alejandro's lawyer and Michael's influence had helped him beat the bogus attempted murder charges, he was no longer sure that any monetary reward was worth the risk—especially not to his tentative relationship with his brothers.

He had no idea what he was going to do next, but taking his father's ring had not been a choice.

Again, he tried to remove it. Again, it did not budge.

Michael finished his drink, chuckling. "Funny. First you wanted it enough to steal it, and now you can't give it back if you wanted to."

He slapped his brother on the shoulder and stood.

"Wait," Daniel ordered, objecting to Michael's departure.

"Can't," Michael said, tossing down a twenty to cover the cost of their drinks. "I have a beautiful woman waiting to show me all the best make out spots—I mean, stakeout locations—in New Orleans. I suggest you stop wasting your time trying to take the ring off and just buckle up for the ride. Your life is about to change, Daniel. Whether you like it or not."

* * * * *

COMING NEXT MONTH

Available September 27, 2011

You can find more information on upcoming
Harlequin® titles, free excerpts and more at
www.HarlequinInsideRomance.com.

HBCNM0911

REQUEST YOUR FREE BOOKS!
2 FREE NOVELS PLUS 2 FREE GIFTS!

red-hot reads!

*Harlequin Romantic Suspense presents the latest book
in the scorching new* KELLEY LEGACY *miniseries
from best-loved veteran series author Carla Cassidy*

*Scandal is the name of the game as the Kelley family fights
to preserve their legacy, their hearts…and their lives.*

Read on for an excerpt from the fourth title
RANCHER UNDER COVER

*Available October 2011
from Harlequin Romantic Suspense*

"**W**ould you like a drink?" Caitlin asked as she walked to the minibar in the corner of the room. She felt as if she needed to chug a beer or two for courage.

"No, thanks. I'm not much of a drinking man," he replied.

She raised an eyebrow and looked at him curiously as she poured herself a glass of wine. "A ranch hand who doesn't enjoy a drink? I think maybe that's a first."

He smiled easily. "There was a six-month period in my life when I drank too much. I pulled myself out of the bottom of a bottle a little over seven years ago and I've never looked back."

"That's admirable, to know you have a problem and then fix it."

Those broad shoulders of his moved up and down in an easy shrug. "I don't know how admirable it was, all I knew at the time was that I had a choice to make between living and dying and I decided living was definitely more appealing."

She wanted to ask him what had happened preceding that six-month period that had plunged him into the bottom of the bottle, but she didn't want to know too much about him. Personal information might produce a false sense of intimacy that she didn't need, didn't want in her life.

"Please, sit down," she said, and gestured him to the table. She had never felt so on edge, so awkward in her life.

"After you," he replied.

She was aware of his gaze intensely focused on her as she rounded the table and sat in the chair, and she wanted to tell him to stop looking at her as if she were a delectable dessert he intended to savor later.

Watch Caitlin and Rhett's sensual saga unfold amidst the shocking, ripped-from-the-headlines drama of the Kelley Legacy miniseries in

RANCHER UNDER COVER

Available October 2011 only from Harlequin Romantic Suspense, wherever books are sold.

USA TODAY bestselling author

Carol Marinelli

brings you her new romance

HEART OF THE DESERT

One searing kiss is all it takes for Georgie to know
Sheikh Prince Ibrahim is trouble....

But, trapped in the swirling sands, Georgie finally
surrenders to the brooding rebel prince—yet the
law of his land decrees that she can never
really be his....

Available October 2011.

Available only from Harlequin Presents®.